"I Love You"
And all the other Lies in Between

Sarah Miller

Copyright © 2024 Sarah Miller

All rights reserved. No part of this book may be reproduced or transmitted in any form or by any means, electronic or mechanical, including photocopying, recording or by any information storage and retrieval system without permission in writing from the publisher.

Bergantino Publishing—Denver, CO
ISBN: 979-8-9886541-0-0
Library of Congress Control Number: 2023945371
Title: *"I Love You" And all the other Lies in Between*
Author: Sarah Miller
Digital distribution | 2024
Paperback | 2024

This is a work of fiction. The characters, names, incidents, places, and dialogue are products of the author's imagination, and are not to be construed as real.

Dedication

I would like to dedicate this to...
    My mom who taught me my love for reading.
    My dad who taught me the value of hard work.
    Daniel who taught me to never give up.
    Hannah who taught me the importance of humor.
    Abigail who taught me to be unapologetically me.
    And all the others in between.

Prologue
Denver International Airport: May 2022

There were, as there are any given day, many different people going to many different places for many different reasons. However, at least for a moment, they were all together in one place, at one time. And then, to never cross paths again.

If you were to look around the airport that day you would have seen quite a diverse group of individuals. Even looking specifically in Terminal 3 around gates C30-C64 in the Denver International Airport you would find a group of individuals who would never have been found in the same area if not for the joined motivation of travel. In the corner near gate C62 you would find a family looking incredibly bored. Or to be exact, three children looking incredibly bored while a mom read, and the father fidgeted. One might see this group and wonder where they might be going. Could it be the graduation of an eldest child from college, or perhaps a funeral of a relative, or maybe even an April wedding. Regardless it was clear the dad had made the decision to arrive with plenty of time to spare "Just in case the airport is a zoo" and arrive with plenty of time to spare they did.

If one were to look around, they would find readers, those watching movies, some working, and others on their phones. In airports there are no rules. Although it was 4 PM, there were some individuals who had flown in early that morning with a layover. Others that were racing to make a flight. Some were drinking at the airport bar, others buying numerous snacks for their flight, and still others perusing the bookstore.

Some distance from the family sat four airline staff. Flight attendants, pilot and the co-pilot. They were relaxing before they would need to head to their next flight. If one were to listen closely, they would hear the pilot and co-pilot discussing the stock market and inflation whereas the flight attendants seemed to be gossiping about a fellow coworker. It would be hard to tell by the casual onlooker however one of the flight attendants was madly in love with the pilot and the individual of which the two were gossiping about happened to also be in love with the pilot. A mile high love triangle.

Right next to the flight attendants, pilot and co-pilot sat a girl. It would be hard to guess her age. She might have been a teenager who was heading off to tour a college for a late visit. Or maybe a college graduate who was flying home. Maybe a lover flying to visit a long-distance boyfriend or still yet flying for a job interview.

She was writing in a journal and every so often looked up to take in her surroundings. She was even eavesdropping a bit on the conversation to her left, with the flight staff. What could she be writing? A love letter? A cover letter? A thank you note? Simply what her day had consisted of?

If perhaps you were the flight attendant to her left, you might have looked over and caught a glimpse of what she wrote. She was writing what happened to be the first entry in a journal. She was writing the following in pen:

4/30/22   2 PM

At Denver international airport on the 1st leg of my journey. Checking in, checking my bag, and getting through security went well. So well that I'm two hours early. I may walk around a bit or maybe get a drink. Next stop Dallas.

Dallas Fort Worth Airport

The Dallas Fort Worth Airport was quiet. At least the gate was. It was around 9 PM in the evening and it was the international division of the airport. This specific gate was a flight set for London Heathrow Airport. Given the time difference between the two, once the individuals about to fly to London landed, it would be around 12 PM in the afternoon. After having flown for 7.5 hours the time difference would launch them into midday. The girl sat, undid the luggage lock from her bag and took out her journal.

This time an onlooker might notice that the journal's cover had a map on the front, etched in the leather of the binding. Perhaps she was traveling? Could she be an exchange student from London who was returning home after a semester or a year in America? Although, from her previous entry little clues would be given to insinuate that she was from London. And, if it was her second entry in Dallas that would make little sense for her to be returning. Therefore, one would assume she indeed was setting out on some kind of adventure.

4/30/22   8 PM

In Dallas, I board for London in half an hour. My whole flight here I kept wondering what traveling with a significant other would be like. I traveled with him but it's different because he wasn't my person. I'm excited to do this alone. I think someday I'll enjoy traveling with my husband/boyfriend but for now I think I need this time to travel alone. Enjoy things alone. See ya in London.

Flight to London

She was lucky. She had the whole row to herself. As she settled in for the long, overnight flight she began to overhear a conversation.

"Girls can get away with just about anything huh?" The comment came from the row next to the girl, a man on the far end of the middle row that some large flights have. He was addressing the woman that was closest to her that was sitting on the opposite end of the large middle row. The woman was donning some type of sleepwear. It was a blanket, poncho type of apparatus. The comment may have taken the woman by surprise or even offended her but the two had been talking for some time before this comment had been made, however the girl had not been attracted to the conversation until that statement drew her attention.

The man continued, "Can you imagine if a man were to put something like that on? My friends would make fun of me for days." The comment may have been construed as rude or perhaps even condescending but apparently the woman paid no mind because she responded with a laugh and a lighthearted remark. The two continued to talk. They both ordered wine and even cheered from across the row to each other. They spoke of the movies that were available on the flight and where each was from and what they did. The girl was a silent onlooker, wondering if she was witnessing the beginnings of a romance. What could be more romantic than meeting a man on the plane and beginning to talk and then flirting and then getting each other's numbers and then from there…

As is the way with airports and flights, the girl never knew what would happen with the two because after the overnight flight had landed and they all had deboarded she was never to see them again. Perhaps as of this day they are married. Or it could be that they dated for a bit and broke up. More likely they never spoke after the flight or if they did it, it likely fizzled out eventually. But to the girl, their future was whatever she made it, and, in her mind, they were happily dating with a winning story of how they met.

London Heathrow Airport

5/1/22   2:19 PM

I landed 2 hours ago in London. My flight takes off in around 5 hours. Security took forever to get through. I didn't realize how strict Europeans are for removing liquids from the bag. I keep forgetting where I am until I hear British accents. So many languages too. It's an airport so obviously but just different to hear so many languages. I slept the entire flight and had my own row. I ended up checking my other bag in Denver which was convenient. Things are about to get real once I land. I'll need to get my checked bags, get a taxi, and head to the hostel. Once I get to the homestead things should settle down a bit.

As she wrote this an older gentleman sat down next to her at the bar. One could suppose by now that she was at least 18 given the espresso martini she sipped as she wrote. Perhaps even 21 given that she mentioned getting a drink when she was in Denver but again it would be hard to say. She looked young and yet there was something in her eyes that suggested she was older than one might assume. Deep in her eyes was reflected something that comes with time. Not sadness or anger necessarily, but rather a kind of disillusionment.

"Where are you from?" The elder gentleman asked the bartender. He was clearly American given his accent.

"I am from South America actually," The lady responded. She was younger than the man by at least a decade.

"Sí, puedo hablar español. Viajo… for work," The older man said in broken Spanish.

The girl's face grimaced without her meaning it to. Secondhand embarrassment for the man and with sympathy for the woman.

The lady responded in English with, "Well there you go."

The woman had a mesmerizing demeanor. Her skin was gorgeous and although it was easy enough to ascertain that she must have been at least in her 50s she appeared little over 30 given her unwrinkled skin. Her accent was enticing and her voice melodious.

The man was now talking about how Spanish women

were the prettiest women in the world. A compliment perhaps but the girl still felt embarrassed on the behalf of Americans everywhere. She was told by multiple school advisors that when she went to Europe she would need to be on her best behavior. They all said a similar thing, "You are now not just an individual going to Europe. You are a representative of the United States. You may be the only person that someone meets from the United States or at least the first person someone meets. You are now responsible for not only the image you portray of yourself but the image you portray for your country."

There was truth to that. She had heard from many people that traveled to Europe from the United States that Europeans didn't like those from the United States. Although that was broad to say. Europe is a whole continent, and it was presumptuous to say that every single European from every single European country disliked Americans. She had been told by one of her friends from Madrid that many Europeans viewed Americans as ignorant to the world and with absolutely no sense of style. She had been told this as if dressing in athleisure clothing was as bad, if not worse, than being ignorant.

She continued to listen although she had long since lost hope that this man would be able to save the conversation. The woman was clearly busy, and he was clearly wasting her time. She finished up her espresso martini and if one were to have looked over her shoulder, they would have seen her type into safari: do you tip in the UK? To which she found out that it is indeed not typical, and people usually round up if they are going to tip. She couldn't help it and tipped more than they had recommended on the website.

5/1/22   5:45/17:45

My flight takes off in an hour to Spain. I'll try to write in this @ the hostel. Things are beginning to feel real. Time to be the best version of myself.

If one were to have read this excerpt one might be left wondering quite a bit. For instance, why was she going to Spain in May. What exactly does the best version mean and what does that look like? However, it is to be noted that this short entry was written at the bottom of a journal page and therefore she simply did not wish to elaborate given that she did not want to begin writing on the next page. If she were to have continued or perhaps ventured onto the next page, she may have written something like this:

This semester was hard. I feel as though I lost a part of who I am or who I want to be. I feel like for the past few months I have been going through the motions without truly being happy or authentic. Now's my chance to change that. Now's my chance to go to Spain and reinvent myself in a way. I want to be more like the best version of myself. I want to each day strive to be the most authentic, hardworking, kind person that I can be. It's hard to look back and realize that this last year I am not proud of the person I was. But this is my opportunity to change that.

Spain

She sat in front of a window at the homestead. Colorful buildings, flowers of every color, and palm trees were the view right outside the window. It was like a painting one might wander up to in a gallery except instead of stumbling upon it in an art museum it was a real-life view seen from a small bedroom in a Spanish apartment. She wrote the following in her journal in Spanish, but it is roughly translated into English below. As she wrote she continued to marvel at the scene outside.

5/2/22

I arrived in Spain last night at 11 (23) at night. I couldn't write because I was in a room with 5 other people. One thing about hostels is that you should not stay in them if you're a people pleaser. I felt so bad about being loud that all I did was go right to sleep. The Uber driver from the airport told me, "Me gustaría tomarte a un restaurante o la playa. Todas las cosas son gratis. Y entonces puedes practicar tu español y puedo enseñarte." I awkwardly laughed because I wasn't sure what to say in response, but he took that as I didn't understand. He took out google translate and showed it to me in English. I didn't have the heart to tell him that I understood but that I didn't know exactly how to respond. It was an interesting way to arrive.

The woman at the homestead is very friendly. She's a bit older and has extreme pride for her country. She speaks of Spain with such love. I walked with my roommate near the beach. The buildings are incredible. Colorful apartments and palm trees and colorful flowers hanging on balconies. I have never lived near the beach and to be so close to the ocean is amazing.

I can't believe that this is my home for a month. I wish that I could stay here longer. Maybe forever. I have a lot of emotions right now. I feel almost overwhelmed with all the possibilities. I think I may have packed too many clothes in my suitcases, but I guess sometimes it's better to overpack.

Each time I look around me I feel like I'm in a dream or a character in a book. As I write this I'm sitting in front of a window and there are palm trees and incredible architecture, and I am finally in Spain. I honestly can't believe it. I feel overwhelmed with emotion and excitement, and I am grateful for this opportunity. I don't even have words to describe how I feel. Thank God for security in travels.

5/2/22   9:55/21:55

At times during today I thought, "What time is it at home?" But it doesn't really matter since I'm no longer there, even so, I still think about the time difference. Not because I want to go back to the US or be with my friends, but because it's an interesting thing. It's interesting that I am here. My family and friends are there. Distance and time make me feel worlds away and incredibly disconnected. To be completely transparent, when I arrived in Spain, I thought all my problems would disappear. As if school, my career, my family, and my friends would pause until I returned. As if my ex-

boyfriend would no longer exist and as if my life would be perfect. This is not the way of life.

In the morning I will try to wake up at 7. I have class at 9 and after that, I don't know. But it's going to be rainy tomorrow so I'm not sure how much we'll be able to do anyways.

We went to the city center today. My roommate and I couldn't find an Uber and didn't know that you could only buy a bus ticket with Euro coins. There is a building there that only has one tower while the other tower is unfinished. Apparently during the US Revolutionary War, Spain gave money to the US and couldn't finish the building. So now it stands there one towered. Incredibly beautiful an awe-inspiring despite its unfinished nature.

March 16, 2022

What is zoom? If you were to go back in time and ask someone from before March 2020 what zoom was, they would probably respond with something like, "Zoom is what makes things get bigger on your computer or phone." Or maybe, "Zoom is what you say when someone is running fast or a car is going by quickly" or perhaps, "Zoom is what you refer to as the fastest lane of traffic on the highway. You call it the zoom zoom lane." Few would have responded with, "It is a program similar to Facetime that allows groups of people from around the world to communicate via video chat." Many things have changed since the pandemic. So many things have happened that no one could have ever dreamed of before March 2020. Sometimes it feels fake. Fake like a made-up dystopian future envisioned by an author that has just enough romance mixed in to keep each reader enthralled enough to turn the page and potentially end up making four movies rather than three which would have sufficed given that it was a trilogy.

She sat with her AirPods in while listening to a woman speak about studying abroad on zoom. The woman had covered insurance, necessary medical clearance, transcript transference and had even been so brave as to discuss being safe regarding drugs, alcohol, and sex. The lady had said, "When you're abroad you tend to think less logically. Just be safe. Don't do anything stupid. Just because you're in a different country doesn't mean you're invincible."

The lady continued, "You should never go abroad trying to escape something. I know I did. I went abroad after my parents died and I thought that by going abroad I would be able to forget or at least I would be busy enough to fill the space that was left in their passing. I was wrong. If for whatever reason you're going abroad in the hopes of curving an addiction, filling an emptiness, escaping a death, or avoiding your problems, just know it's not possible. Get the help you need here and now because going to a different country will not solve these. If anything, it could make it worse." The lady began speaking about other information and although it may have been important, she was already thinking of other things. She was not trying to escape anything in particular. Or maybe she was… She kept telling herself though that she simply wanted to improve her Spanish and see more of the world. And eat a lot of Spanish food of course.

Now, a few months later she sat in the room of a Spanish apartment. Writing in her journal before heading off to class.

5/4/22   8:17 AM (Antes de Escuela)

With each trip, vacation, or each time you meet a new person there are expectations. We have hopes, ideas, and dreams about trips and people. Expectations can be a little bit dangerous, or they can be very dangerous.

I think about my expectations. My expectations of the people in my program, Spain, my classes, and I realize that I had a lot of expectations. But, more important than these expectations, I have a lot of things I would like to achieve.

I think that a balance of experiences is important. I want to have a fun experience, lay at the beach, be with friends, and enjoy my time here. But also, I would love to learn more Spanish and have more opportunities speaking Spanish and listening to Spanish. I guess that's life in general though. Learning to balance life and work, fun and travel. I think it's something I may never fully master.

21:43

Today was a day of reflection, realizations, and thinking. I walked by the ocean and as cliche as it sounds, I realized that I am learning more than just Spanish while I am here. I am learning about Spain, the culture, the people, and maybe most importantly, I am learning about myself.

For example, sometimes I forget that I am insecure. I forget that I want everyone to like me. I want to make friends and to do well in school. And here I am, a little sad because even in Spain I still have insecurities and I still have a little sadness. For all my life I have wanted to fit in. Just because I'm in Spain doesn't mean that's changed.

And right now, I feel a little bit of disillusionment. Not because Spain is horrible, or I hate it but because I'm realizing that no matter the distance from home. Some things always follow behind. The insecurities I have felt my whole life unfortunately don't just disappear with distance or time. Likewise, the past is always there despite distance and time. Sometimes I wish that it was simple. As simple as time and space to erase the past. To forget certain things. But that's not possible. It never will be.

As she (I) sat in the small room in a Spanish apartment. Her (my) thoughts went back to her (my) past. Not just to what I had left behind recently but to my childhood and all the things in between. I thought of things I would never write in that journal. Things that are still too painful to write. Too painful to even think about. Regardless, my mind went back. Back to it all.

Part 1
The Budding

June 2015

The days dripped into the next. Dripping like the popsicles they licked on the front porch when the sun was directly above, watching it slowly drip down into the leaky horizon. The sun oozed like honey pulled up out of a jar as the sun peaked out and morning began, rays streaming down and caressing the town. Afternoons were hot. Sticky like melted ice cream. The nights. The nights leaked by slowly at first. But with greater velocity as time moved on. That was how the whole summer felt. Dripping morning into afternoon and afternoon into evening, one day into the next.

Summer is like a favorite t-shirt that is originally too big. As time passes the t-shirt begins to fit better and better, sometimes the t-shirt is left on the shelf for months as winter treads footprints across time. Every instance the t-shirt is donned, it feels different and eventually it doesn't fit at all. The feelings of fondness felt don't fade but wearing it never quite feels the same. That's how it is with summer. Expectations and excitement are felt leading up and as soon as summer is tried on, it doesn't feel better or worse than the year before, just different. But it is never the shirt that changes, it's the person wearing it that does the changing.

She sat on the front porch step, licking the popsicle. The street was busy. Cars driving slowly, stuck in tar. She adjusted her shirt. Too tight. She pulled down her Levi jean shorts. Too short. Her thighs sticking to the porch. Cars stuck in tar. Thighs stuck to porch.

As her teacher liked to say, "Puberty is a time when young men and women are budding. Blossoming into the young adults they are meant to become."

In her teacher's mind humans are like plants. Planted by parents, birthed when poking through soil, growing, growing, growing, and then budding, and then eventually blossoming. That's how her teacher explained it, "Girls bud breasts."

She budded last summer. Her small, tender buds slowly grew throughout summer and winter and spring and had now blossomed as spring flowed into summer.

Puberty seemed delicate, exquisite, and beautiful when her teacher described it. Girls and boys portrayed like innocent plants, growing, and budding, and blossoming into beautiful flowers. Experiencing puberty didn't seem delicate. Didn't convey exquisiteness. Appeared quite far from beautiful. Anything but innocent.

Puberty was sticky. Her body didn't seem to bud gently, rather, budding hurt. Ripping away childhood and all the ignorance that comes with it. It wasn't natural like growing a plant. It was awkward, it was painful, it was embarrassing. It didn't feel like budding. If anything, it felt more like shedding. Shedding an old skin. Shedding like a snake sheds its scaly skin, slithering away, leaving it behind.

It was abrupt, however. As abrupt and anticipated as a blossom. Perhaps her teacher was right after all. Blossoms are stared at. Coveted. Talked about. Wanted. A passerby gazing at the beauty might walk on and forget all about the blossom, a passerby might even crouch down and smell the blossom, a passerby might go so far as to hold the blossom, the passerby might even pluck it right out of the ground. Regardless. At some point the passerby will lose sight of that blossom among other blossoms and eventually lose remembrance of it at all.

The cars continued to ooze bye, the popsicle dripping, afternoon fading to evening, and her blossoming.

Static

She stood up. Her thighs needed to be ripped off the porch. She turned around and began walking towards the front door. She heard a call from traffic and turned, expecting to see a friend, an acquaintance, or a familiar face. Rather, the oozing traffic was at a standstill. She stared across the waves of traffic to see not one face she recognized.

"Look at that ass. Let's see you turn around and walk away again." The voice came from the closest wave. A pickup with windows rolled down, two mid twenty-year-old men. She quickly turned around and walked to the door. Ashamed that the one thing they asked was the only thing she had thought to, or even could, do. She ran up the steps to her room. Vehemently closing the door, throwing the popsicle stick on the ground, clawing at her shorts to pull them down, tearing them off eventually. She stopped, catching her breath in the darkening of her room. The sun rays escaped through the curtains and slithered across her naked legs.

She remained standing in the middle of her room. Shorts discarded next to her bare feet. Her cheeks were hot. Warm from the sunshine outside, painted pink from her run up the stairs, flushed from the words. She felt disgusted. Her body felt sticky. Was it wrong to hate the words and the men and yet feel almost excited? She felt gross. The words sticking to her. The realization that they saw only her body. The newness of it. Yet, excitement by the recognition that she had power. If that's what you called it. Power that is completely helpless. Power like a flower that a wasp flies to. The wasp chose the flower. The flower is completely unable to control who or what looks.

She grabbed a pair of loose shorts. Slipping them on as the sun faded lower and released her legs. She walked downstairs, late afternoon hanging heavy around the house, singing fading melodies of the day as the sun sank lower.

She smiled at her mom as she jumped up to sit on the counter, watching her mom make dinner.

"How was the day?" her mom asked, the sizzling of bacon filling the kitchen.

"Good. Uneventful," she responded looking out to the busy street. Legs dangling and swinging. Distracted by her thoughts. Like the cars driving along the street, as soon as one thought drove by, another followed.

Listening to the sound of the bacon sizzling, her mind went back to the sound of the TV when it was off channel and the static rose up and filled the room. She kept thinking about the sound of the static and the...

"Would you mind setting the table and calling down your sister?" Her mom's voice cut through the static and the static changed back to bacon sizzling once more. She jumped down from the counter and started grabbing plates from the cupboard.

"Where's dad?" she asked, placing the silverware on the table.

"Working a bit late. He said not to wait up." She looked at her mom, seeing something hidden behind her words.

I lay in bed staring at the ceiling. I'm in Spain although my mind had just been wandering far away from where I am now. My mind had slipped miles and countries and year back. I'm sticky from the heat despite the light breeze wafting through the open window. I hear the sound of the ocean waves as they hungrily creep up the shore, just to retreat and come back once more. I don't want my mind to go there. Yet the darkness is impermeable. The air is hot, the darkness heavy. I try to stop the thoughts from surfacing, I try to delay the images that come to my mind. But I am helpless to it. Helpless then, helpless now. The darkness clears and it's as if I'm once again her.

TV static. She was young. She couldn't even remember how young or old. All she could recollect was she was not even close to budding. She didn't try to remember the events, rather they came unsummoned from somewhere even deeper inside her than the darkness that surrounded her.

She was sitting in the basement, playing with toys. That's what kids do, play with toys. The basement was dim, and she was alone. Her mom was somewhere with her friend. Her younger sister was safe in her mother's arms. And she was alone, in the basement, playing with toys.

She heard footsteps but didn't bother looking to see who it was, playing all the while. Her mom's friend's son had come downstairs. She didn't remember how old he was. Older than she by many years. She smiled at him but continued playing, just a child playing with toys. She was confused as to why he was here with her; she was a kid playing with toys, didn't he have something better to do? Somewhere better to be? Doing something older kids do rather than play with toys.

He sat down next to her. She couldn't recall what he said or if he said anything at all. She continued playing with her toys. He reached out to her. She didn't say anything. Young. Unbothered. Confused. He slowly put his hand down her pants. Strange, she thought, for him to put his hands where she used the bathroom. She didn't say anything. She felt awkward. Uncomfortable. What was she supposed to say? She was young, he was older. She continued playing with her toys, hoping by continuing playing it would end. He would go away. He would stop whatever he was doing. She played with her toys, and he played with her.

I push the thoughts away. Push the thoughts away although the image of his hand on me plays as if the darkness is a TV screen. I try to run from the feelings I had felt but the hot, heavy air holds me hostage. The darkness is too bright. The hotness is too heavy.

The ocean waves seem too loud. As if at any moment they will reach up to me and drag me with them as they recede and pull me under.

I bite the inside of my cheeks. I want the pain to scare away the feelings those memories cause. I was young then. I didn't know it was wrong. I didn't tell anyone. Who could I have told when I felt strangely ashamed? What would I have said when I hadn't understood what had been done?

I bite harder. Tears welling up in my eyes, but it's not from the bitten cheeks. All those years ago my teacher had said that puberty was like budding and blossoming. But what happens before the budding and the blossoming? What happens to a flower when, before it buds, it's stepped on. What happens to the flower when careless feet tread on it and curious eyes inspects it. What happens when hands touch it, wondering as to what it might be like once it has blossomed. What happens to the buds then? What happens to the blossom?

Does the blossom feel ashamed, afraid of the looks of the passerby. The blossom wishes to be unseen. Unseen by a stranger, unseen by a known, unseen by all. Does the blossom hide amongst the other blossoms? Does the blossom pretend nothing happened at all? It's not as if the blossom has missing petals. The blossom appears untouched, fresh, and beautiful. Why not pretend it so?

Part 2
The Blossoming

Perspectives

She hurtled down the hill. The wind suffocated her as she pressed past it. The wind tore her face open. Her eyelids forced back so that tears escaped and dragged across her face. She wished the hill would last forever. She didn't have to think about the top or the end. She could be anyone in that moment. No worries, responsibilities, or obligations. Just a girl hurtling down a hill.

She braked sharply at the light, the squealing of her bike wheels forcing her from her reverie. First day of her job. Glamorous. Hardly.

She parked her bike. Walked into the restaurant. The day began.

Hostessing and then eventually serving, a profession stretched ahead of her for as long she would want it. But in her mind, it went like this: Host, school, serve, school, college, serve, college, serve, graduate, and never serve again. "Hi, how's it going? How many? Any kid menus? Inside or out? Ok, right this way." Over and over and over. Walk with menus. Come back. Repeat. Again, and again.

What she liked most was going outside. When the rush lulled, she'd take any excuse to clean the patio tables and even sweep or clean up trash from the grass. Summer teased her those first few weeks. Stuck with "How's it going. How many? Any kids? Inside or out? Ok, I can take you right this way." The patio tables mocked her. The sun kissed her cheeks, and the wind pulled her hair until she had to return inside. Summer winked at her when she cleaned the trash from the grass, the trees overhead creating gnarled shadows that embraced her body and traced shadows on her legs and arms and neck.

Two long weeks passed. Each day seeming the same as the day before. Summer dancing before her without her being able to dance along. Two weeks. Then a break.

A Tuesday morning. A breeze pushing through her window, playing with her curtains. She opened her eyes knowing today was the day she'd been waiting for. She felt something, opportunity, change? Didn't matter what. Today was a break and she was going to make the most of it.

Ripe. Beginning of summer. Full bloom.

She made breakfast. Toast. Avocado. Simple. A cup of tea. She headed to the front porch. She sat on the porch swing, placing her food on her lab and the cup of tea on the side table. She crossed her legs, adjusting the plate, and let the sound of cars passing and birds singing fade out the loud sound of her thoughts.

Summer. A beginning. An end. The new. The old. Blossoms. Roots.

She didn't want extraordinary. She wanted something new. She didn't want something breathtaking. All she wanted was something different.

She put her dishes away and raced up the stairs two steps at a time. She opened her dresser, grabbed a pair of shorts and a white shirt.

She took some money and headed to the bus stop.

In that time of life, adolescents experience what is referred to as "adolescence egocentrism." The concept where they feel as if they are the center of the universe. As if they are the main character of the play or the star of the movie. All eyes are on them. Every action, every word, everything is seen, watched, and criticized. They are the main character, and all others are audience members watching and waiting for the show.

She might as well have been.

Everywhere she walked she felt as though eyes were constantly glued to her. Every look was eternal. At every whisper she was the center. She felt watched. She felt investigated.

She might as well have been.

The bus driver sat at the bus stop, waiting impatiently for a group to step onto the bus so that he could drive them where they needed to go so that he could turn around and do it all over again. Impatient to get started with the endless.

A girl walked onto the bus. Young but not young. Full and ripe. Wishing to be unnoticed and yet impossible to be inconspicuous.

The bus driver eyed her up and down. He could tell she was trying so hard to be unnoticed and trying so hard to not see him see her. She was trying hard to not see anyone see her.

She was sitting at the front of the bus when she saw her walk in. A pretty girl. Long lashes. Long hair. A natural beauty. She just wished the girl was more covered up. She should know better, she thought to herself. The white shirt was see-through to the point where you could see the lacey, light pink bra that peeked through the white. A rose hiding amongst the weeds. She could tell the girl hadn't realized the see-through nature of her top. There was a distinct difference between girls who did that on purpose and those who did it completely unintentionally.

The jean shorts were short. Short enough so the girl pulled them down when she walked onto the bus. She could tell the shortness made the girl uncomfortable. She could tell that the girl could feel the eyes and she could tell the girl was trying hard to avoid the eyes.

She saw the girl walk onto the bus. She scoffed. She was her age. A slut. No mistaking a try hard. The girl was wearing the shortest pair of shorts she owned no doubt. So short she might as well be wearing nothing but underwear. She could tell the girl felt her staring, she pulled down her shorts. She scoffed. She was acting as if she were embarrassed by the shortness, but she knew better than that.

She was wearing a pink bra. It was obvious that she wore the bra so that it could be seen through her white shirt. The combination was well known. Bright colored bra and light-colored shirt. She might as well have worn nothing but underwear and a bra. She looked straight out of a Victoria Secret ad. She rolled her eyes and fixed her eyes on the road. Slut. She was screaming for attention.

He looked up from his newspaper to see her get on the bus. She was in high school. Looked about the age of his daughter. He would never let his daughter leave the house like that though. He shook his head. Where were her parents to let her go out in public like that. They were basically asking for their daughter to be stared at. Her shorts were short, and her shirt was see-through. He almost wanted to get up and tell her to go home and put some clothes on. Why did girls that age insist on taking hot weather as an excuse to wear nothing? If he ever saw his daughter trying to leave the house like that, he would sit her down and tell her to change. What happened to modesty? What happened to clothing? His mind wandered to the ripped jeans his daughter had bought that winter.

He looked at her and said, "Where are the rest of them?"

She had said something about fashion, and he really wasn't sure why you'd pay more for less but what did he know…

She walked onto the bus. She felt as though every pair of eyes had shifted to her. She pulled down her shorts. They were basically the only pair that fit her. She should've worn jeans, but she'd put most of those away for the summer. Besides, who wears jeans in the summer?

She ignored the eyes. She was sure that she was just imagining them. She walked towards the back of the bus. As she walked to the back, she recognized a dad of one of the girls she went to school with.

His daughter didn't have the best reputation when it came to school. People were judgmental. She tended to wear less perhaps in the spirit of less is more. Regardless, she always admired that girl in that she insisted that her style was an expression of who she was. Who could judge someone that was so unapologetic? She was a pioneer to her. Disregarding dress code and wearing ripped jeans. Unfortunately, many argued that her self-expression was nothing short of whorish. Poor girl.

She sat near the back of the bus. In a seat alone to get away from the eyes. She had considered sitting next to a girl her age but had continued walking anyways. She turned her head to look out the smudged window.

Grown Out

We grow out of old things. We grow out of old t-shirts that we once wore daily. We grow out of friends that we once said would be our forevers. We grow out of love with those we once saw the future reflected in their eyes. We grow out of ourselves. We grow out of who we once thought we were. We grow out of past selves and past dreams and past bodies. We grow and we move on. Sometimes it hurts, sometimes it's painful. But without fail, we grow.

She jumped out of the bus, pulling her shorts down once again. She felt too large for her body. She felt as though she didn't fit. She felt as if she had outgrown herself to the point where she felt uncomfortable in her own skin. Like a plant that outgrows its pot, she felt as if she needed to move on to something bigger, less confining. What was it that she needed? She wasn't so sure. She walked along the street, intermittently pulling down her shorts. The cars were loud. The bustle was busy. The sound of humans took over. She could be anyone she wanted at that moment. She could be meeting a friend or buying a bike or meeting with her mom for some shopping. What was she really doing? Growing out.

She aimlessly walked around for a while, taking it all in. She knew when she saw it, she'd know. And she did see it and she did know.

She pushed open the door. The harsh bell of the store sounded, revealing her to the rest of the shop. An eager employee who was bored from the slow morning attacked her,

"Looking for anything in particular today? I can help you out if you need. Everything on the left side of the store is 25% off as long as it's on the pre-approved list. Otherwise feel free to look around and let me know how I can assist you."

"I'm ok for now, thank you. Just looking."

She was just looking. But she was looking for something specific. Something where she'd grow up or grow out or fit in. Although she may have been "just looking", she was "just looking" for something that could transform her.

She wandered among aisles of clothing. "Just looking" for something.

She found a dress. It was a beautiful dress. Flowy. Light blue.

She found a pair of shorts. Not too long. Not too short.

She found a pair of jeans. Loose and comfortable.

She found a shirt. Clean. Simple. Tight.

But what did she want to find?

Did she want to find a dress where she would be hidden? Hidden among the flowiness. Lost in the blue.

Did she want to find the perfect pair of shorts? Not too long and not too short. Enticing and yet modest.

Did she want to find jeans where she could seek comfort? Non-confining. Filled with ease.

Did she want to find a simple shirt? Bland and safe.

What did she want to grow out of? What did she want to grow out of and into? Did she want to grow into hiding or grow into finding. Did she want to wither or did she want to bud. Did she want to grow in the shadows where she was rarely seen or did she want to grow on the top of a hill where all eyes were on her. Did she want to embrace the eyes or sulk from them?

There are many stories focused on a turning point that affects the life of the main character. A choice that defined them and made them who they are and where they end up. But there isn't always one, single, pivotal moment. No bildungsroman. Humans are rarely defined by a single decision. They are made of a million small ones. For her this was one of those moments but not to be confused with *the* moment. There is no such thing as *the* moment.

It wasn't about finding the perfect pair of shorts or the perfect outfit. It wasn't about finding the shoes that fit too well to pass up. It wasn't about an outfit; it was about deciding how she wanted to be seen. Did she want to hide? Did she want to stand out? Did she want to be in the shadows or on the hill? Did she want to grow out into the world, or did she want to grow in?

It wasn't solely about how others would perceive her; it was about what and who she wanted to be regardless of what others would think or say. She had spent too long feeling too big for her own skin. Uncomfortable and confined. She was ready to feel confident and comfortable and unapologetic.

She took it off the shelves. Headed to the counter. The worker was still underwhelmed by the business of the day.

"Did you find everything ok?"

"Yeah, I think I did. Thank you."

She grabbed the bag. Headed to the bus stop. She went to a coffee shop first. Bought the first thing she saw.

Drank it quickly. Headed to the bathroom. She ripped off the shorts and threw them in the trash can. She tore off her shirt and lacey bra and threw them away as well.

She put it on. Took a deep breath. Fixed her hair. Looked at herself in the mirror. She had grown out of the shorts. She'd grown out of the lacey training bra. She'd grown out of who she once was, innocent, not yet having budded. She had grown out, but she could never grow out of her memories.

She looked in the mirror one last time. She wished she could throw away some memories as easily as she'd thrown away her shorts. She wished she could wash the memories down the drain. Wash them away like the dirt that was washed from recently gardening hands. She sighed. She couldn't get rid of them; they were as much a part of her as her very skin. They were roots. Roots that were necessary in order to grow, in order to bud, in order to blossom. Without her memories, even those she wished she didn't have, she wouldn't be here. She wouldn't be her. She wouldn't have grown out without those memories.

She picked up her wallet and picked up her memories and without even a glance at the discarded clothing, she walked out of the bathroom. Not new. Not changed. Just grown out of.

I wake up. The sun streaming in. Another day of school. My time in Spain is passing faster than I would like. I enjoy the clarity I get from being in Spain. Time and distance between who I once was and who I am now. I get ready for class and think back to that girl. The girl I once was. Even the parts that are hard to think about, the parts I would rather forget. As I go through my day, I try to stop myself from thinking about things I'd rather not remember. But as I take a late-night walk along the beach my mind slips back to that night. A night I wish I could forget.

Part 3
The Picking

Dirty: May 2018

Alcohol swirled through her head like the smoke that swirled around the party. The music was loud, the darkness was bright, the room felt humid, and she wanted to find her friends. It was hard. Hard with the darkness clouding her head. She tried to get her phone unlocked but was struggling to type in her password. She was drunk and she wanted to go home.

"Hey. How have you been?"

She looked up, hoping to find one of her friends but was disappointed when it was a boy she used to talk to. Not even date. Talk to. They'd hooked up once.

"Oh hey. What's up," she said, still trying to unlock her phone. Looking around the party again and trying to find her friends.

"Come with me," was his response.

"No thanks, I'm just trying to find my friends," she replied as she began to walk away.

"Oh c'mon. Just come with me." He grabbed her shoulders and began walking her to the front door.

"No. I just want to find my friends."

He didn't respond but kept walking. She tried to

pull away. But the alcohol made it hard. Made it hard to stand. Made it hard to walk away. Made it hard to do anything but follow without wanting to follow.

"Please I really just want to find my friends." She tried to pull away once more. They were already at the front door. She looked around trying to find anyone.

"Just for a little. C'mon."

She didn't want to.

They got to his car.

"I'm going to go find my friends."

"Stop. Just come here for a little."

They got into the car. She tried to text someone, but he had grabbed her face. Kissing her. Sloppy. Sticky. Wet. His breath smelled of weed. His breath smelled of alcohol. His hands felt wrong on her body. His lips felt wrong on hers.

"Please no. I just want to go back to my friends." She had pulled away from his grip. His grip was hungry. His grip was unapologetic.

"Why not. We've done it before."

"I don't want to. I want to go back to my friends."

She fought to find the words to say no. She fought to pull away. She fought against his lips and hands. The hungry hands. The hungry lips. If he wouldn't listen, all she could do was give in and then leave. Then maybe he'd let her leave. She just wanted to leave.

But he didn't stop there. He kept trying. Refusing to listen to no and stop and not now. Why wouldn't he listen? Why didn't he listen?

She felt dirty. Ripped from the ground and trampled.

She felt like a flower in a garden with a sign that read "Please do not pick." But someone had picked anyway. Then dropped and left. She felt misused. She felt sick. But most of all, she felt dirty.

It wasn't the kind of dirty that can be washed off. It wasn't the kind that could be fixed with a shower. It wasn't even the kind that could be fixed by scrubbing and scrubbing and scrubbing. Because she'd tried. She'd tried with cold water. Hoping the coldness would make her feel pure once again. She had tried scalding water. So hot she'd hoped it would burn the outer layer of her skin and take away the grime and the dirtiness with it. She had sat in the bath, scrubbing, and ripping and clawing at the dirtiness. Regardless. It remained. It remained despite all her efforts. She was left if anything, feeling dirtier than before.

She had this feeling in her heart. She felt this ache in her head. Her whole body felt like ice. As if someone were to even look at her, she would melt. As if someone were to tap even gently, she would crack. She felt empty. Like a hollow carcass. As if someone were to knock on her, they would only hear an endless echo. Her eyes felt like mirrors. No emotion. No response. Just there. If anyone were to peer in, they would see nothingness. Nothing but their own reflection staring back. Nothing of her and her own hopes, feelings, dreams, only a reflection of them. Of their hopes and dreams and thoughts. She was an empty shell. A wilted flower. Maybe not even a flower anymore, a dirty weed.

What gave someone the right to make her feel this way. So unclean. So faded. So torn up. Her body felt strange. Like a home that was locked up tight. Windows cracked to let in the breeze. Curtains open. Like a passerby deciding to stop and peer into the blinds. Deciding to break in through the locked door and enter in without permission. The house unable to stop it. And then, the passerby to leave and close the door behind them so that those who follow after seeing the house and it appears unchanged. Unchanged except for the curtains are now drawn shut and all the windows closed tight.

I remember what I felt like after that night. Sometimes I still feel it. Even here. Even now in Spain. Oceans away from that place and that person and years away from who I once was.

I remember feeling as though I was too dirty to find anyone. I remember not wanting to find anyone. I didn't want to be touched ever again. Being touched brought it all back. Sometimes it felt suffocating to think about that night. How my body became a stranger, and my mind became a prison. I try to forget. It's not possible though.

I had thought I was too broken to find someone. I had convinced myself that I didn't want to find someone. That was until I met *him.*

Part 4
The Trampling

July 2021: When We First Met

It was a warm summer day at the end of July. The kind of deceiving summer day that makes you feel as though summer would never end. On a day like that, I felt as though it never would. I had worked in the morning and then taken a run outside, soaking the sun into my skin. My friend and I made plans to go to dinner at a restaurant with a patio so that we could enjoy more of the sun and long summer day.

I pulled on a skirt, accompanying it with a cropped, white shirt. No need for a bra. As we walked out the door my phone rang. I answered it to a crying friend. Not necessarily the best start to the evening. We arranged to pick her up to come to dinner with us. As the three of us drove to dinner, my friend divulged the details behind her tears: boys. Apparently one of her guy friends had made a particularly offensive comment at her expense to which she did not respond well. I quickly comforted her by saying that he probably had no intention of hurting her feelings as, "That's just how guys are." That's just how guys are.

We soon forgot about boys and offensive comments as we ate salads on patios accompanied by cold beverages in the warm descending sun. My previously crying friend easily convinced me and my friend to go and get a few drinks before heading home. How could a day like this end so early? Why not stay and elongate the day by a few harmless drinks?

Typically, when someone tells a story about "When I first met them" the story takes on a life of its own. Perhaps changing day to day or depending on who's asking or soon becoming exaggerated beyond reality. The telling of when I first met *him* has always remained more or less the same. On a beautiful day at the end of July, when the sun was shining, and summer seemed unending.

I hardly remember the beginning of the night. Not because I was drinking but because that's how it is sometimes when an event happens. One may not remember what happened before or after, but they distinctly remember that one, specific event.

I was driving and therefore not drinking much, and as it so happened still under the age of 21. Not that it mattered. I had long since lost my fear of using fake IDs after having an early introduction to the bar scene soon after turning 18. The first thing I remember after dinner and entering the bar: dancing. I love to dance. When I go downtown, all I want is dance. Dance with my friends, dance on top of bars, dance with men. I love to dance. Something about the music and the lights and the human experience as everyone moves to the same sound waves.

I was dancing. I was dancing with my friends on the dance floor as the music pulsed through our eardrums and the lights flickered with different colors. The air was thick with music and sweat and sound.

It was then, while I was dancing that I saw *him*. As the lights faded in it out, he emerged through a group of dancing people. Tall, dark, and handsome. The generic recipe for disaster. But what's the matter with dancing? Dancing is innocent enough. Besides, he had a presence to him. I don't know how to describe his presence. It was the presence of someone who doesn't care. Someone who doesn't care what people think of him. I couldn't help but dance with him, as if he were a magnet pulling me closer. Pulling me through the throngs of people and swirling bodies towards him.

It turned out my friend knew him. She encouraged me to dance with him. I remember how natural it felt. He was tall and I was short but wearing heels so that we were the perfect fit. His hands were large. Large hands-on hips as his hands traced their way up from my hips to my chest. I remember blushing. Blushing by his hand placement. Very aware in my mind that I was not wearing a bra. Very aware that these strangers' hands were on my breasts, breasts with no bra, in a crowded bar. It felt natural though. His hands weren't invasive but rather exploratory. Introductory. Testing the waters. I calmly guided his hands back down, where they remained. Unapologetic, back on my hips. I could've danced with him for hours. Our bodies moved well together. Like the way water from a river meld into a larger body of water. Natural. Unobtrusive. Seamless. Liquid. Liquid mixing with liquid.

I was jolted from the dancing by my friend and one

of his friends asking us to come grab a drink with them. All things must come to an end at one time or another, so I complied. I remember perching on my knees on the bar chair. I didn't want my bare legs touching the coldness of the bar chair.

"Could I get your Snapchat?" he asked me. It made me want to laugh. The question. It seemed almost juvenile. I have always had something against Snapchat. It offends me in a way. It's impersonal. Sending random pictures to someone else. Pictures that they probably send to 20 other people.

"No. But you can have my number," I replied.

"That's even better. He'll take your number," his friend interjected.

"Oh, I'll take your number. But I won't text you for four days." *His* dark eyes twinkled as he told me this.

His friend and I shared a look. I rolled my eyes. His friend and I said in unison, "Why four days?"

All he did was shrug his large shoulders and smile. He had a nice smile. Pearly white teeth. Almost perfectly straight. Almost perfect but not perfect. Sometimes perfect is too unnatural anyways. I preferred his smile to a perfect one.

The dancing and conversation are burned into my memory like someone took a brand to my brain. Some of the events in between became a little muddled with time but what happened next is incredibly clear. I was standing with my friends when a man approached me, "Can I buy you a drink?"

To which I simply replied no and explained I wasn't drinking as I had work in the morning, but I would take a water. The man left with a rolling of his eyes and not even a single word in response. Rude, I thought to myself. A few moments later, *he* appeared by my side. Not the can I buy you a drink guy. But *him*. He handed me a water.

It would be almost embarrassing to recount such a bland, boy meets girl at bar story. I would be tempted to change it to something a little more exciting or a little cuter. But to me, how we met was perfect. I can't explain the feelings I felt. The way we fit so perfectly. The way he knew exactly what to say and exactly what to do. The way he handed me the water with no words, no explanation. Knowing that he had seen the exchange between me and the other man. Noted what I wanted. Gone and gotten water. Done all of it without expecting anything. Boy meets girl in bar but boy cares enough about girl to notice. To some it may seem simple or unoriginal or perhaps even common sense. But to me, in that moment, it meant a lot.

That's how we met.

4 Days Later

I'm not sure how it is with all people. But when I meet a guy, I get excited. I wake up and am thrilled by the possibility of what the day might bring and the conversations that might be had. Of course, I meet a lot of guys since I'm in college, but I don't always get all that worked up about it. Typically, when someone asks for my Snapchat, and I'm not interested, I'll give it to them and not add them back. But if I am interested, I will give them my number.

Unfortunately, I don't have a great track record

concerning guys I have given my number to, or first dates, or second dates for that matter. One guy took me to a bar and then his friends ended up showing up and joining the date. Bizarre in general. But then one of his girl friends was mean to me the entire time. More bizarre. Then, he acted like the date had been great. There was never a second date.

Another guy I wasn't quite interested in, but he had been incredibly sweet, and I wanted to give it a try. He asked me questions and cared about what I was doing and introduced himself to my friends when he saw them at the bar. One time he even let his friends leave him so he could spend time with me at the bar. We had a second date. But there just wasn't anything there. I really tried to give it some time and give the "good guy" a chance, but there wasn't a spark.

Another guy made me dinner on the first date. The dinner was quite delicious. We watched a scary movie. We even shared a magical kiss. We went on a second date. For whatever reason, the entire second date I was dreading kissing him again. I knew I would have to. Especially when he paid for lunch. I kissed him. Walked back to my house and I never talked to him again. We had nothing in common. He hunted. I'm not a fan. He wore cowboy boots and was "country" and I'm a "city" girl who likes fake nails and dressing nice and has never owned cowboy boots.

Another guy took me out. The dinner was lovely. He was funny. He was nice. He was smart. We got along well. I enjoyed our conversations. We had things in common. There was a spark. We watched a movie and as we watched it his arm naturally went over my shoulders. He explained the parts of the movie I didn't understand and hugged before he left. I was excited about him and... he ghosted me. He never talked to me again. That was a blow to my self-esteem. I kept wondering what I had done wrong. What had I said to ruin it? I must've done something because the date had gone perfect.

Still another guy, we didn't even make it to dinner on the first date. I had seen him around campus and had thought multiple times about how handsome he was. We ended up meeting at the bar one night and he got my number. We texted for a few days. Then we didn't talk for a few days. Then he finally asked me on a date. He chose sushi. I would say always trust men who choose sushi on the first date, but I can't really agree with that anymore unfortunately. He came to the door. He even opened the car door for me. Unheard of. I remember thinking: Chivalry isn't dead. I had just buckled my seatbelt when he asked me a question. The answer to the question was yes. Although I can't disclose what he asked me due to legal issues/HIPAA, long story short, the date was illegal. So, I unbuckled my seatbelt and walked back to the house. It had started raining during the time we were in the car, so I had to run into the house and ended up soaking wet. We never spoke again.

I should mention that I almost always wear the same thing on first dates. I'm not sure why, but I have discovered the classic first date outfit and have never been able to find one that is superior. I like simple things. So, I go with dark jeans. No rips. Skinny because I'm not quite gen z and I like the sophistication. I wear black booty heels. Steve Madden naturally. My roommate's white shirt with a push-up bra for classy cleavage. Depending on the season I will add a jacket over top. Gold earrings. Gold necklace with green pendant. Simple. Pure. Classy. Pair it with a black purse.

With *him* it was different somehow. He had left an impression. I talked to my friend about him, and she explained that they'd gone to high school together. They had never been friends or run in the same circle, but she said that he was well liked. She told me that she didn't know too much about him but that overall, she'd heard he was a nice guy.

I waited without realizing I was waiting. My phone would ring out a notification and I was sure it would be him. Just for it to be a text from a friend about her ex, an email from a coworker asking if I could cover a shift, or a text with an image of my dog from my mom.

"He did say he'd wait four days," I told my friend.

"Why would he wait four days?"

"I don't know. That's just what he said."

"That's weird."

"I think it was his way of being mysterious or playing hard to get."

"Yeah, I guess. But that's still weird. Especially to say it to that person."

So, I waited.

Day two hit. Then the end of day two. I couldn't believe his audacity. To actually wait four days. Who does that? I was working when I went over to check my phone near the end of my shift. An unsaved number had texted me. I smiled. It was him. I don't remember the text, but the gist was something like,

"Hey, how are you? So glad to meet you the other night. What have you been up to today?" Something along those lines. To which I responded, "Couldn't resist talking to me for four whole days huh?." He didn't respond. 10 minutes. A half hour. An hour. I left work. No response. I got home.

No response.

"He's probably going to wait four days to respond now. Why did I say that?" I told my friend. She just laughed and shook her head. But as we were talking, I received another text. From *him*. So started a month and a half of texting. Texting about days. Texting about lives. Texting about work. Him and I were super busy, so I wasn't perturbed that he hadn't asked me to hang out yet. We both worked multiple jobs. Besides, I was about to go on a trip for a few weeks and there was no time to see him before. So, we continued texting.

I was flattered. Flattered that he enjoyed talking to me. Flattered that he was continuing to talk to me regardless that there was no possible time for us to hangout in the foreseeable future. He must actually want to get to know me, want to take me out. I was thrilled. I was excited. I couldn't stop talking about him.

"So, I met a guy."

"He's tall…"

"Dark hair…"

"So handsome."

"He's a hard worker."

"He actually asks me about my day."

"We haven't been able to hang out yet."

"He's super interesting to talk to."

So, I waited some more. This time it was not for a text but for the opportunity to go on that first date.

The day was hot. Oozy. The kind of day that is sticky and melty like a popsicle left too long in the sun. The day had come. The day I would hang out with *him.* I had long since planned the outfit I would wear. Obviously. Since I always wear the same thing on first dates. Casual, but not *too* casual. Flirty but not *too* flirty. White top, jeans, heels. Simple and to the point. Like me.

I waited anxiously. He had said 7 PM but wouldn't tell me which restaurant we would be going to. The mystery worked just as well for me. I liked a good surprise. He pulled up and I could hear his music escaping the confines of the truck he drove.

He didn't come to the door. Strike one. You always expect the man to come to the door. At least I do. I'd let it slide this time though. I had told my friends that since he's 6 ft. 3 in. that I would ignore three red flags. That's the rule: For each additional inch above 6 ft. the man gets free red flags. I have now since changed the rule. For each inch above 6 ft. the man begins with that number of red flags. He must make up for those inches above 6 ft. because those inches typically seem to correlate with more red flags than the typical under 6 ft. male. As if being tall allows a man to be an asshole.

I let the text come through. Brightening the screen of my phone with possibilities and newness and excitement. "I'm here." First date kind of excitement. I waited. Sprayed some additional perfume. Did some last-minute adjustments to my outfit. Smiled one last time in the mirror and exited my front door.

There's etiquette to a first date. For example: The man picks the woman up **on time** (he was a few minutes late). The man comes to the door and knocks (which he hadn't done). Part of the etiquette for the woman comes from the door exiting. For example, if he had come to the door (like he should have) I would always be sitting in the living room with my friends. My purse would be set close by the door, but not too close. If he had knocked, my friends and I would've sat a moment, before I would walk slowly to the door. Greetings would be shared, my purse would be grabbed, and with a goodbye to my friends I would let him lead me to his car.

With the current scenario. The waits-in-car-and-texts-scenario has a similar etiquette with a few key differences. I was given the benefit of an additional perfume spray, lip gloss plump, and any other adjustments. This makes him wait an appropriate amount of time for me to exit the house. As I exited the house, I turned a moment to call out to my roommates a quick goodbye and a smile. This is important. The first thing you want them to see is you turning around with a smile, clearly having said something to the people within the house.

Although I am an expert on exiting-the-door-etiquette I don't know if I've ever mastered the etiquette of walking to the car. Who has? Do you look at them through their car window? Do you appear to glance at your surroundings? Do you look at your phone as if you had just received an important text? I went ahead and walked straight to the passenger side door, hoisting myself up into the truck.

"Hi, how's it going?" I said, with a smile.

"Not bad. You look good," he said, matching my smile with a charming grin. I hate the word grin but there's really no other way of explaining his smile. It's almost irritating. It was the irritatingly attractive grin of a man who knows he is attractive. His grin seemed to imply that he was handsome, and knew it, that he was in control, and knew it.

"Thank you. You look good yourself." I could continue to recount the pleasantries we exchanged but there's really no point. I have never been one for small talk. I am much too serious. I don't really care about what you ate for lunch or your mother's maiden name or the color of your childhood home. I would like to know the color of your pets though.

As we drove to the sushi restaurant, which was an excellent choice on his part and which I had previously considered a green flag, he had his window rolled down. Although I should have considered my hair, which I had meticulously curled to appear like a blow out, I quite literally threw caution to the wind and rolled my own window down as well. And suddenly the sun seemed to be shining even brighter. I was sitting in the seat next to a handsome man. Windows rolled down. The wind caressing my face. I felt as though I was in a country song. Nothing but possibilities. Nothing but moving forward. Nothing like a first date.

Although I was not 21, I managed to get a drink. Something light and sweet and girly. He later told me that this was one of the first things that impressed him. My ability to get what I wanted even when I am not supposed to.

A seasoned sushi eater, I used the chopsticks to eat my food. To give credit where credit is due, he did attempt to use the chopsticks for a good five minutes but only managed to get a few morsels of rice in his mouth. Finally, he succumbed and used his large hands to eat it. This image might bring to mind something grotesque or messy, but he somehow made eating sushi with his hands seem like the only possible way to eat it.

Something about him intrigued me. Maybe it was the way he carried himself. He carried himself as though he knew that everyone was looking. Which maybe they were. As I've mentioned a few times he was tall, dark, and handsome after all. I liked the way everyone looked when we walked in. I was small, blonde, dainty, petite. Using chopsticks and finessing underage drinks. He on the other hand was tall, manly, rugged, and dark. Using his hands to eat sushi. Somehow it worked though. Eating sushi with his hands seemed to be just part of him. Unapologetic.

His stories made me laugh. He told stories well. I have never been exceptionally good at telling stories. As a child I hadn't always been popular. Other kids oftentimes left me out or lost interest in me quickly. Throughout middle and high school I felt as though if I took too long to tell stories, people would stop listening. Because they often did. I soon became the one to listen. So, I listened. I almost felt lame in comparison to him. He had all these incredible and funny stories, and I was very cut and dry. How many interesting things could I disclose given my upbringing? Suburban middle class. School. Sports. College. Eventually grad school on the horizon.

That's me. Meanwhile he had stories of his family, epic fights, run-away horses, almost catching on fire but being saved by a baby, robberies, of going to prison because of a sandwich, and spring break trips getting apprehended by border patrol.

I was mesmerized. His voice was like the ocean. Strong but melodious. Loud but not ashamed. He was what he was. He is what he is. He owned his past. Spoke with excitedness of his future. Seemed to live quite in the moment as he did not look at his phone once. Great first date etiquette by the way. But, beyond all else, he was unapologetic as to who he was. I liked that.

We talked for hours. Time seemed to slip by too quickly with him. Before I knew it, I was in front of my house, listening to him talk in his truck. I kept looking at the clock. It seemed to be deceiving me as it read out 10:27 PM. I wanted to keep listening to him. I wanted to hear his voice and feel his presence and I wanted to keep looking at the way his lips moved. I wanted to hear his laugh and listen to the way he talked about everything with such zest. I liked the feeling of tension. Wondering if he'd reach out to me. I kept wanting him to pull me in with his large hands and kiss me with his lips.

He walked me to the door. Walking to the door after a date is very proper etiquette. Trying to get inside? Terrible etiquette. He told me one more story about dancing with a goldfish and said goodnight and turned back to his truck. I was just about to open my door when he turned me around, grabbed me, and without hesitation, kissed me. That was the first date.

Outside and Insides

The clock was ticking. Every few moments I would look at the clock. It felt like when you watch water boil, or when you're watching grains of sand sift through an hourglass. Not that I can say I've spent much time watching sand in an hourglass or sand sift through an hourglass for that matter. Each tick of the clock seemed to be hitting my eardrum louder and louder. Finally, the time dismissed us from class. Some class about policy. It would be just as boring as it sounds except for the professor.

He was amazing. Passionate. Good at teaching. Interesting. He often graced us with stories about weekends of running over 20 miles. How he managed to run that far in a day was beyond me. I don't think I've ever run 20 miles even within a month. Although that description may make him seem even less interesting, he truly is one of the best professors I have ever had. He inspired me to pursue my dreams, demonstrating that if you love what you do, you truly don't have to work a day in your life. I wanted that for myself, to find the intersection between where passion meets purpose. The idea that you should find what your strengths are, find where you can allocate those strengths to create a better world or make a change, all while enjoying what you do. I never wanted to wake up, dreading my job and feeling as if I wasn't making a difference.

He had told me he wanted to see a waterfall. He had moved somewhat recently and didn't know as much as I about the local hiking areas. I had a hike that I enjoyed. Not even a hike. More of a walk. It was paved and less than a half a mile in total. So, once the clock finally ticked enough for class to be excused, I texted him and then we were off to hike.

"It's kind of hard. But don't worry, we can go slow and take as many breaks as we need to. I'll bring plenty of snacks and water. Trust me, the waterfall is worth the view." I had told him. I wanted to get him nervous before he'd realize that the "hike" was nothing more than a 10-minute walk. A little joke.

We walked and talked and reached the waterfall in no time.

"Some hike huh?" he asked, laughing.

"Did my Adidas give it away?" I replied kicking up my foot to observe my shoe wear. I had made the mistake of wearing blue Adidas on this "very intense hike."

"They were a bit of a giveaway."

We stood, his arms around me, staring up at the waterfall. The water cascaded down in slow motion. Fierce and powerful yet controlled. We stood there and I knew I would never forget the moment. The summer turning to fall. The trees changed to bare as the leaves floated to the ground. The mist from the waterfall on my face. His large arms around me.

As we walked back down, I hopped onto his back, and he carried me. We passed by an older couple. As we went by them the woman said, "Remember when you could do that with me." The rest of the conversation was carried away, but I smiled thinking about the future. Thinking of remember whens.

"I bet that poor man will not hear the end of all he used to do for the rest of the night," he joked.

As we drove back into town he spoke of his

dreams. He talked about he wanted to tell his kids one day of all the adventures he and their mom had gone on. I agreed. Did I mention that I loved his stories? Stories about the things he wanted to do and the things he had already done and all the things he was doing. At times I felt as though perhaps he didn't care so much about what I was doing or what I was going to do just because he talked so much of his plans, but I knew that wasn't true. He did care. That was one of the reasons I was drawn to him in the first place, he did care and because of the conversations we had.

I loved his stories, but I also loved our discussions. We didn't always agree on everything and were both stubborn. We'd had conversations on psychology, childhood, and differences between genders. Occasionally politics. Again, we didn't always agree but I enjoyed hearing a separate opinion at times. I felt like my brain would grow when we had these kinds of discussions. I enjoyed them.

I enjoyed that he liked my passion. I could go on and on about childhood and the impact that childhood experiences have on development, and he was equally interested to hear what I had to say. I loved talking about books I had read or was reading, and he would tell me the same. He had early on shown me this book he was reading, *The Art of Seduction.* I had heard of the book but never read it so he would tell me about what he had read so far. I joked that he must've used the advice from the book on me. He just smiled his charming smile and told he didn't need a book for that. I shook my head at that although I knew he was right. He hadn't needed a book for that. One night as he sat on the edge of my bed, he had pulled out this book to show me and told me he highlighted important things from the chapters he was reading. He flipped open to a page and the entire page was highlighted.

"That page must've been exceptionally important huh?" I said with a smile. Him and I laughed and laughed and laughed.

We both loved reading. We had read a lot of the same books as kids and seemed to have similar interests as far as genres. I'm talking *Hunger Games, The Lightning Thief, Harry Potter.* Those books are somewhat popular in general but even the less popular books we seemed to have both read. We had both read *The Alchemist* in school and he told me how much he enjoyed that book. I had never fully formed a sophisticated opinion on the book but loved when he spoke about it.

He brought me a book one day. A spiritual book. He told me that he had read that book more times through than any other book. I told him I typically read the Bible if I wanted to read something spiritual. Within the week he told me he had bought a Bible. I never did get around to reading the book he gave me and looking back, I doubt he ever actually bought a Bible.

That's what was so exciting. We both loved reading, both had read similar books, both enjoyed talking of the books we were currently reading. We had different opinions but appreciated hearing each other's viewpoints. I never tired of hearing his stories and loved telling him of the things I was learning in school. I liked that we didn't need to be on our phones. I enjoyed that we could have meaningful and intellectual conversations. I appreciated that we didn't have to agree. I liked that he wanted to see waterfalls and go on hikes with me. I liked him from the inside out.

A 21st Birthday, a 1st Disagreement, and a LARGE Rumor

I was turning 21. The day I had long awaited was happening in a few short days. There would be a party, festivities, cake, my siblings would be coming into town, and I was beyond excited to finally be able to legally drink and get into the bar. Although I had been illegally drinking and illegally getting into bars since the ripe age of 18.

He wanted to take me to dinner. We had gone to an Italian restaurant early on when we had first met and had decided that it would be our place. Our go to celebration spot to celebrate important things. We had been dating for a few weeks but "talking" for over two months by the time my birthday came around.

The night began with him being late. Not atypical. But we always managed to get to our reservation only a few minutes late and never missed them. I was slightly annoyed since he was late so often. I hoisted myself into his truck, and he began talking about work and this and that. I couldn't understand why I was getting slightly annoyed. After all, I typically enjoyed listening to him talk about work and what he was planning on and what he was working on. But, for whatever reason, perhaps a combination of him being slightly late, school pressures, and the arrival of my siblings on the horizon, I felt irritated. He must've sensed my irritation; he typically could sense my emotions like that.

"But enough talking about work. Tonight, is all about celebrating you." As those words slipped from his lips I immediately felt better. We ate bread and calamari, drank wine, and discussed my siblings coming into town. I had some apprehension just as we hadn't been dating long. I wanted *him* at my birthday of course but I wanted him to know that my siblings would be there, and he would be meeting them and that I was a little nervous and my brother was really protective and my sisters occasionally intense and might ask about intentions and… But he just smiled and let me know that he was excited and of course he'd be there and he was excited to meet them and that this is what relationships were about. I felt better and again calmed down.

I drank a bit too much wine. He drank a bit much wine. We both drank a bit much wine. We drove back to my house. I wasn't convinced he should've been driving, but he insisted he was fine. I can't quite remember what brought on the argument or why it escalated but we got into an argument about a word he used. You may think, what word could he possibly use that would create an argument. Well, words have importance and I at times can be annoyingly particular about being "politically correct." I got upset at a word that he used that he definitely should not have.

"I would prefer if you wouldn't use that word around me, please." He took offense to that. We had a discussion.

"I'm just going to go home. I have a meeting," he said.

"Look, I just don't want you to say that word around me. I'm sorry if I came off as rude or demanding but please don't go home. Besides, you don't have a meeting, it's 9:30 PM."

I began to cry. I had drunk too much wine and his reaction had surprised me and I was upset that he wanted to go.

"Don't cry. I will stay. I'm sorry. I'm just surprised. This is the first bit of emotion I have ever really gotten out of you," he comforted me. I didn't like feeling vulnerable, but I was also surprised that he had commented on my emotions. Throughout our time together I thought I had been doing a good job of being open with him. I hadn't been given a reason to cry in the relationship before. Well, except that one time. But that time didn't count because we weren't dating then.

The night ended well enough. A stupid thing to have fought about anyways.

I don't remember my 21st birthday much. This seems to be somewhat typical for 21st birthdays. The day had been busy, and I didn't start drinking until I got to the party my friends threw me. Then, I drank way too much way too fast. I don't remember much but I do remember my friend saying she didn't like *him,* and I remember crying. That's more or less all of it. I do remember one other thing, at one point one of my friends was talking to me and all I said was, please get *him.* I just want *him.*

He made me feel safe in a way that not a lot of other people could. When I was stressed, I knew he would know exactly what to say. If I were sad, he knew the best way to cheer me up. I remember feeling upset that night and not wanting anyone but him. Not wanting anything more than to be with him. To let him hold me and tell me it would be ok. I'm not sure what made me upset, just that he could make it better.

No one told me much about that night. No one seemed to be able to tell me why I had started crying. "I just drank way too much way too fast." Is all I said whenever anyone asked about that night.

"How sweet of him to take you home and take care of you," my sisters said to me. It had been nice of him. It made me feel protected and taken care of. Not to mention, I had been so drunk that I had forgotten my phone in the Uber. The Uber driver lived an hour away. *He* drove my siblings to the airport and then he drove me to get my phone from the Uber driver. No one had ever done those kinds of things for me before.

He had taken care of me drunk. Gotten me out of my birthday clothes, which happened to be quite confusing with all the ties and loops and things. He had checked on me as I threw up in his bathroom, held me close despite my puke breath, and hadn't been angry when I woke him up in the middle of the night once I had finally become less drunk to ask what had happened. Then he went to brunch with me and my siblings and then took them to the airport and me to my phone. He truly was so selfless and kind.

It must've been a few weeks later that I got a phone call from my brother. *Him* and I had gotten brunch and then I was heading to fill up my car with gas and bring him to his truck. My brother called and asked if I was alone. I said yes assuming he was asking because he didn't want to interrupt anything. He rarely called so I didn't want to tell him I was busy.

The conversation quickly took a turn I had not been expecting. So, when we reached the gas station I stepped away from the car while *he* filled up my car with gas. Basically, my brother was telling me what happened the night of my birthday. Apparently, all my friends had at one time or another, approached my brother and told him how they didn't like *him.* Which caught me off guard. None of my friends had ever stated any concerns to me. Many of my friends had even said that they liked him. But what my brother said next made my heart sink. That weird feeling when it feels like your heart is freezing and your whole body feels like it's falling down out of yourself and through your feet. He told me that one of the girls at the party had told everyone how *he* had cheated on me just a few days before. I couldn't believe that. How could *he* have done that? How could anyone do that and then meet your family? Who could do that and then go and celebrate their girlfriend's 21st birthday with all her friends? My brother continued to say that none of my friends had told me because there was no proof except for this one girl's word and apparently, she had rescinded ever having said anything. I stood there, listening to my brother talk and watching *him* fill up my car. *He* was watching me, knowing something was wrong based on my face.

I couldn't believe that *he* would do that. How could anyone do that? My brother continued to talk and explain that I should proceed cautiously in the relationship even if there was no proof. He gave advice and said many other things, but I didn't hear any of it.

I said goodbye and took a deep breath. *He* had gotten into the car. He had pumped my gas for me and had paid for it. I couldn't believe that someone who had done all those things for me would have cheated before meeting my family. Taken me to dinner. Listened when I told him my fears and worries and comforted me. Driven hours to get my phone. Bought me beautiful gifts and written sweet notes. How could that person do something like that days before meeting my family and then go to a party like nothing had happened.

I walked over to the car and sat in the driver's seat. My whole body shaking.

"What's wrong baby girl? Is everything ok? What did he tell you?"

I tried the entire time we drove back to his truck to work up the courage to say what I had just heard. I needed to ask. I had to know. I didn't know how to say it. I was crying at this point.

"Just tell me what's wrong. It's going to be ok," is what he told me.

"I will. I just need to park the car first," I responded. I took a deep breath and looked at him, "My brother called me and told me that at my birthday everyone was told that you cheated on me a few days before."

I let the breath out. I was watching him closely to see his reaction.

"I knew something like this would happen," he replied. "That's not true. I would never do something like that. People just like to talk and create drama and mess things up when they see other people happy."

"Yeah, but that girl said it was her friend. And the girl who said it is my friend. Why would she lie?"

"Why did she tell everyone except for you? If she was a true friend, she would've told you. Not told everyone except you."

I can't really remember what else we talked about. I almost felt bad for doubting him. He was so hurt that someone had said those things. He felt horrible that I had for even a moment had to think he would ever do something like that. I shared with him how this was tough on me in particular because I had been cheated on before by both of my previous exes. I told him how my ex had messaged a girl asking her to come over the day before he met my dad. I explained that this was especially painful because he had just met my siblings. He reassured me and told me he was sorry this had happened.

He dropped me off at my house where I did homework while he picked up food for us. As he walked in, he said, "Look, I just wanted you to see for yourself. I would never want you to doubt this."

He held up his phone where there was a Snapchat message from the girl he had allegedly cheated on me with. He had asked her, "When was the last time we hung out?"

And she responded with, "Idk the fourth of July."

I felt better. But sad. Why would my friend say those things if they weren't true? Why had none of my friends told me? Why did this have to complicate a relationship that had been going so well?

I sit on the bus heading downtown. I have a good 40 minutes right to the city center. Some people are listening to music, some reading, and others talking quickly in Spanish either on phones or to the person sitting next to them. My mind thinks back to *him.* Someone that two months ago had been my everything. Despite our occasional fight or the unfortunate rumor, he was the most thoughtful man I had ever met. I couldn't help but compare him to my ex or other men I had talked to. Everything that they had lacked, he had. He texted me good morning every morning. He never hesitated to tell me how he felt about me. He told me I was beautiful. He held my hand whenever we were in public, hugged me goodbye whenever he was leaving, and he brought gifts for me and my roommates. He bought me dinner, made me dinner, and always made sure I had eaten. He was funny, kind, and thoughtful. He was everything I was looking for. He was everything I had been missing.

But of course, things change. Every story has more than one side. He has a side; I have a side. But regardless of the side. Things changed slowly.

The Good, the Bad, and the Ugly

Things were going well. We were both busy but still made time for each other. During the day we each would go about school and work and other responsibilities. Usually around 9 PM he would come over and we would spend time together. He would wake up around 5 AM and I would lay and watch him while he got dressed and ready for work. Then I would get up around 7 and begin my day.

We would text each other throughout our days. Checking in with each other, asking how the day was going, and sending each other funny things on Instagram. Then, on the days we didn't see each other, we always made sure we had plans on when we would see each other next. At first, we did not see each other much during the weekends as we were both too busy.

But eventually we started to spend more time together and he would always visit me when I worked on the weekends.

My heart would flutter when he would come in and suddenly, I wasn't doing such a great job at serving because he was there. Sometimes I would stay at his place, and he'd drive me to work and pick me up and then we'd spend the rest of the day together. We worked out together when we could, we watched movies and discussed the plots together. We went out with my friends on the weekends to the bar.

Before we had even started dating my car had been having issues. I went to the shop and ended up having to be there way longer than I had anticipated. *He* took his lunch early and showed up and brought me lunch and hung out with me for a bit. I'll never forget the mechanic telling me once *he* had left that, "I can tell that man loves you so don't go breaking his heart."

I remember thinking: This is what relationships are supposed to be like. We each were busy, we each had work and school, we each had friends and family. But we made time so we could spend it with each other. We worked to do what we could to make the other happy and share our lives together.

Whenever he came over, he would bring me something. The first time he ever came over he brought pizza for me and my roommates. He would bring me popsicles that I had mentioned I liked and not just for me but for my roommates as well. Whenever he was on his way over, he would ask if I needed anything. Sometimes I did and sometimes I didn't but regardless he often brought over little snacks or even meals when he knew I hadn't eaten yet.

He would spend time with me and my roommates because he knew my friendships were important. So, sometimes we would watch a movie downstairs (this was rare, but I knew he was trying). He would talk to my roommates and go out with us to the bars. On Halloween I was supposed to go to a party with him, but my friend wanted me to go to a different one and he was understanding and met up with us later. The morning after Halloween as we headed off to brunch, he mentioned that my friend and her boyfriend should join us. It was his idea. It made me happy that he was trying so hard.

He made sure to see me at work on the weekends whenever he could get his lunch break. He came to support me for things that were important for me and comforted me whenever I had academic struggles. He would tell me that I could do it and that I was strong and smart and capable.

He met my uncle early on. A few weeks after meeting my siblings. We all got dinner and drinks. My uncle and he hit it off. Talking and drinking. I sat and watched and smiled. That night we all drank a bit too much. We ended up not going out with my friends but rather going back to his place. We were both tired and had already drunk too much. On the way to his house in the Uber as I rested my head in his lap, he told the Uber driver, "She's the most incredible woman I've ever met. I care about her so much. She's tired so we need to get her home. She is everything to me." He leaned down and kissed my head.

He had been planning on going to a wedding for a while. I remember him telling me early on when we first started dating that he had a wedding in the fall. The date approached but a few days before he started acting weird and told me he wasn't going anymore.

I remember that I had sent him a typical good morning text and he had responded with one word. Very unlike him. So, I asked him if anything was wrong and what I could do and if he needed anything to just ask me. He told me that he wasn't going to the wedding anymore, and I asked why. He stated that he didn't want to be put in a position where what we had would be jeopardized. I was confused by this. Why would that be the case and what was he inferring? To me it sounded like he was implying that going to this wedding could put him in a position to cheat.

Anyways, he came over that night so that we could talk about it. He explained that he was the plus one of a girl friend (He said girl friend and not girlfriend) from high school and that it didn't seem right to go. I told him that I agreed to some extent but that if it was just a friend, I didn't want him to miss a wedding just for that reason. I told him that I trusted him and if he wanted to go that he should. His friends would be there, and he knew the people who were getting married so he should go. He explained that it wasn't that he thought *he* would do anything. But when drinking is involved, and other girls are around he didn't know what *they* might do. I told him that it was kind of him to think that way but that he had control over his behavior regardless of whatever they were doing. It ended with him saying he would rather not go at all. I told him if he wanted, he could absolutely go but that I appreciated him declining based on his thoughtful reasoning.

Weeks later I booked a flight to visit my friend for

her birthday. I would go there after I spent Christmas with my family. He had bought a flight to celebrate with his friend for his birthday but that would be in early December.

We were sitting in my bedroom when I told him, "I bought a flight to see my friend today!"

"Why?" is all he said.

"So I can visit for her birthday. I'll go after Christmas and spend New Year's with her."

"I wanted you to come with me to visit my family. We talked about this," is what he said in response. Which, to be fair, he had mentioned this a few times. But he had always said he wanted to go before Christmas, and I had told him I didn't think that was possible for me.

"What if I went to visit her and then we flew out to see your family? It's her birthday so not only do I want to, but I should go and see her. Besides, she flew out for my birthday."

"I just don't get it. She wasn't even that nice to you on your birthday so why fly out and see her? Why don't you just see her when she comes back to visit sometime?"

"Because it's her birthday and I want to celebrate with her."

"So, you're going go to visit her and mess around with other guys?"

"Why would you say that? Of course not. I want to celebrate her birthday. She also has a boyfriend. Why would you even think I would do something like that?"

"I just don't think going to see her is a good idea. Based on what she was like on your birthday I don't think you should go."

"You're going to see your friend. I could make the same argument. I don't get it."

"It's different."

"How is that different? We're both going to celebrate friends' birthdays."

"It's just different."

I'm not sure how the conversation ended. I can't remember what the consensus was. All I know is the next day I brought it up to my friends.

"He said that he doesn't think I should go and see her for her birthday."

"Why?"

"I don't really know. He basically said that she hasn't been that good of a friend to me. How does he even know?" I didn't feel like mentioning what he had said about messing around with other guys.

"Exactly. You've been dating him for months and you've been friends with her for years. No matter what happens between you two, you know that she will always be there. He can't say the same."

"I just don't think he's in a position to say those things," is all I said.

I kept thinking about it all day. Confused on why he cared. Confused on why he thought it was different. Confused why he would make a comment and act like I would ever be messing around with other men while we were together. I would never do something like that.

After my classes I went to his place. I walked into his house, went to his room, and sat down on the bed. He walked up to me and put his hands on my cheeks so that he was holding my head. He was holding me gently, making sure I was looking at him.

"I'm sorry," is all he said. His beautiful brown eyes

looked at me with the utmost sincerity. His eyes searched mine.

"About what?" I asked.

"It wasn't fair of me to act like you shouldn't go see your friend. You should. You absolutely should. It's her birthday and you guys will have a great time. I'm so sorry if I came off in a way that I shouldn't have."

He kept holding my head in his hands. He continued to apologize, "I need to work on thinking things through before saying things. I'm sorry for making you feel that I don't trust you or that I am trying to control you in any way."

"That's ok baby. I was just confused is all. I understand why you might feel that way."

"I was thinking. Let's fly out and see my family after you go see her. I actually have a buddy that lives near your friend that I have been meaning to go see. I wouldn't go see him at the same time of course."

"Why not? You could visit him. I could visit her. Then we could fly together to see your family. I can talk to her and make sure she doesn't mind."

"Really? I don't have to. I was just commenting that I have a friend who moved there."

"No, it would be fun. Besides you could hang out with him, and I could hang out with her and then maybe we could meet up if we're able to. It would be nice for you two to meet again and maybe get along better." I said with a laugh.

I called my friend and she said that it would be fun if he came out. She even suggested that maybe we could all go out together for New Years. I looked at him and smiled.

"Why are you smiling?" he asked.

"I'm just happy," is all I said. Because I was happy. He made me happy. We made time for each other when we could. When we had disagreements, we talked it through and figured it out.

My friends and I had planned a trip a few hours away. We were going to spend the weekend at my uncle's house and stay there Friday and Saturday night. While we were there, he had decided to visit his family that lived a few hours away.

We began our Friday night by going out to dinner with my uncle. I had a few drinks at dinner and from there, we went downtown. We jumped from bar to bar. Seeing people we knew, meeting new people. I sent him texts and videos through the night, knowing I would want him to do the same if he were going out without me.

I was drunk once we got back to my uncle's house. I was eating cake and making snow angels on the floor. We all went down the stairs on our butts, making quite the ruckus on the way down. I forget we were young then. Still doing silly things and figuring life out.

I was drunk and wanted to call him and let him know I had made it home safe. I mostly wanted to hear his voice. It made me feel slightly pathetic, I had just seen him that morning, but I already missed him and his voice and his touch.

My friend was also drunk and grabbed my phone from my hand to tell him hi. Although I was tired and my judgment slightly impaired, I could tell that he was annoyed by something. He ended the call quicker than I would've wanted and told me to go to bed.

In the morning I texted him and he seemed fine. We

exchanged a few normal texts and then the texts came through. I can't remember exactly what they said but they were along the lines of how if I was joking around and wanting to be immature then he wasn't sure what we were doing. I was completely confused by his texts and stated my confusion. He inferred that my friends were making fun of him and that I was being immature, sending videos of us at the bar and letting my friend talk to him on the phone. I apologized without understanding what I was apologizing for. I even called him multiple times trying to clear things up but he said the same things about me being immature and treating our relationship like a joke. I had absolutely no idea what he was talking about.

Throughout the day I tried to understand. It was difficult to be with my friends, trying to have fun while I knew he was mad at me. I also couldn't understand what I had done. Later that night I texted him and somehow the conversation shifted. It was no longer about me being immature but rather that I didn't do enough for the relationship and that he cared more about the relationship than I. I was completely taken off guard. We had never really fought before. I had been confused enough with his conversations about me acting immature and now he was making an assertion that I didn't try hard enough and didn't care.

Although I was at dinner with friends, I went outside and called him. Our conversation went something like, "You don't care about me, and you don't really give what I give in this relationship."

My response was, "I don't understand. If you need me to do something else or more all you need to do is ask. I don't think it's necessarily fair to say I don't care enough or do enough, I thought we were in a good place. I had no idea you felt this way."

It went back and forth. Things got to the point where I thought we were going to break up. Eventually I said, "Look, I enjoy your company. I really see this going somewhere but if you're in a position where you don't think I do enough and I think I'm doing all I can, then maybe we aren't meant to be together. I would never want you to feel unvalued. I do value you and I'm sorry if it doesn't come off that way. I'm looking forward to meeting your family and pursuing this. I don't understand where all this is coming from and I'm sorry."

His mood seemed to shift suddenly, and he said, "I'm sorry. You're right. You do a lot for me. I just get in my head sometimes about this. I like you more than I anticipated, and I get in my head about if you like me as much as I like you."

And that was that. I drove back home the next day and we talked a little about our discussion and then continued as though nothing had happened. I still felt disoriented by his comments. They had seemed to come out of the blue. It hurt my feelings thinking that he thought I didn't do enough. I was trying. I thought that I had been giving a lot. I had been making time for him, paying for dinner evenly, and I had even bought him a basket of gifts and gotten us dinner when he got a raise at work to celebrate. I felt hurt and confused by his words but since I had gotten back the whole conversation felt fake. Things were normal. He was happy. I was happy.

We went out to dinner that night, it was a few days before I would be leaving for Thanksgiving. I drank a little. I said something I probably shouldn't have said. But to be fair, I thought it was funny and thought he would find it funny. A guy that I had once talked to came in with a girl. He had told me he was allergic to fish and couldn't come to the restaurant he now stood in. This was a seafood restaurant after all. I told *him* that, thinking he'd find it funny. I said something like, "I find it funny; he must've really not wanted to take me on a date. I'm glad I'm here with you, someone who wants to be with me."

Looking back, I see why he got upset by my comment. It wasn't necessary to point out someone I had once talked to. I would've been upset if roles were reversed, and he pointed out a girl he once spoke to. I would've wondered why he would do that while we were on a date. What I never understood is why he didn't say something then. Instead, he waited to bring it up. And that's when things get ugly.

I had flown home for Thanksgiving since I hadn't gone home that summer. I spent time with my parents and caught up on homework.

I was sleeping, deep in a mist of dreams and wrapped tightly in my covers. Outside it was cold and I felt cozy and secure in my bed. It was my second night being home and I was woken up with the sharp trill of a text message coming through. It must've been around 1:30 AM. He had texted me. I smiled thinking about how he was thinking of me even at this time. I reached over for my phone and felt even more secure and safe. He was miles away and still wanting to check in with me and text me. My smile quickly faded as I read what he had sent. The text read 3 words that changed it all. Funny how words have such power. Power to create things. Power to build things up. Power to foster friendships and forge bonds. Power to destroy everything in a single moment. Power to tear everything down.

They read, "You're a slut." I thought I must still be dreaming or that in my half-asleep state I had misread the text. I looked again but the words were the same. "You're a slut." Bright and ugly on my phone screen. The bright, artificial light from my phone permeating the darkness. Shattering the darkness and shattering my reality. I began to shake. I felt confused and hurt.

I went to Snapchat, he had snapchatted me something along the lines of, "You're a whore and you act like you're not." And then sure enough on Instagram he had sent me a message that said, "I don't know why you act all innocent when you've slept with all these people."

So, here I was, lying in my high school bed receiving texts on multiple platforms from my boyfriend telling me I'm a slut, a whore, and a variety of other equally disrespectful comments.

He said, "I can't be with someone who's a hoe."

I texted him saying things like, "What are you talking about? Don't talk to me that way. It's not true and so unnecessary."

He kept sending it repeatedly. Things like, "It's ok that you're a slut. Just accept it. But I can't be with someone who's a slut."

I kept thinking my eyes were deceiving me. Who says those things? I kept thinking that it was a mistake or some cruel joke. A nightmare and that I would wake up realizing it had all been a dream. A fake reality. Not my reality.

I called him even though it was now after 2 AM. I

heard a voice in the background. He kept hanging up. I kept calling back. Eventually he answered, in the call I heard him say, "Thanks for giving me a ride."

At least I knew he was home safe. I kept trying to talk to him, asking him why he was saying those things. He just kept repeating it over and over, "You're a slut. You're a hoe. I can't be with someone like you."

Eventually I just said, "Look I really care about you and it's breaking my heart that you're saying those things. I'm going to bed because I'm going to church early for Thanksgiving. We can talk in the morning."

In the morning he sent me videos and voice memos saying how sorry he was. He kept repeating how he couldn't believe he had ever sent those things. He said he would never want anyone to talk to his younger sister that way. He said that he was embarrassed and that he had drank too much. I simply replied that I would prefer to talk later in person. I said that I hoped he had a fantastic Thanksgiving, but I needed a moment.

And then, while I was at church, as the choir sang songs and the multicolored light filtered through the stained glass windows, the texts began again. The same commentary, "You're a slut, you're a whore. I can't be with someone like that." The texts kept coming. It felt wrong to be surrounded by beautiful music and colorful light and to be discussing all the things to be grateful for while these texts came through. Each text was like a hammer chiseling away at my heart. Hammering pieces of it away, little by little, chunk by chunk.

I replied after church, "Listen, I don't understand why you would apologize just to keep sending things that aren't true, but I am currently with my family trying to enjoy my Thanksgiving. We can talk about this later. I can't text you right now."

But he kept on sending the texts. Eventually he sent a text saying something like, "Happy Thanksgiving. I don't want to talk to you right now."

All Thanksgiving on his Instagram and Snapchat story he was posting things as if all was normal. As if he was having a great Thanksgiving. Meanwhile I kept forcing a smile on my face in front of my family. I didn't want them to know I was upset. I didn't want them to see me cry.

I kept expecting a text saying he was so sorry. That he couldn't believe he had said those things. What I couldn't understand is why he had apologized to suddenly begin again with his rant. In the morning I headed to the airport, and he texted me even more degrading and hateful things. He even said, "Why don't you have one those guys you're messing around with pick you up from the airport because I'm not going to."

As my mom dropped me off, she looked at me and said, "Honey, is everything alright you seemed sad this weekend."

"No, I'm just tired, that's all. It was so great to see you all. Love you so much." As I walked through the airport and security, tears fell down my face. People could see me crying but I couldn't hold it back any longer. It was better that strangers see me cry than my family.

I attempted to do homework at my gate. I had to ask a friend for a ride since *he* was supposed to get me from the airport. My heart hurt so badly. Who says those things? Who says those things to anyone? Who says those things to their girlfriend over Thanksgiving?

I sent him a long text saying something like, "I

apologize if my comment at dinner made you upset. I never even went on a date with him but regardless I understand that the comment was unnecessary. I am not a slut and you saying those things is incredibly hurtful. I have enjoyed getting to know you and building a relationship. I am confused why you are suddenly saying these things. I don't have a lot to say other than that my heart really hurts. I truly thought that this relationship could become something special."

He didn't respond. I continued to cry as I took my seat on the plane. I had cried throughout the entire airport. I had been struggling to even do homework with the tears blocking my vision. Blotches covering the notes I was taking, making the words become fuzzy and distorted. As I was about to turn my phone on airplane mode, he called.

"I'm so sorry. I feel sick because of the things I've said. I will come get you from the airport."

"That's ok, my friend said she'd get me."

"I told you I would, so I will."

Why did I feel relief? Why did my tears suddenly stop? I should've hated him. I should've been angry that he would ever say those things. But I didn't. I cared about him. I was hurt that he'd say those things, but I really did care about him. All I could think about was all the memories and all the things he had done for me. Showing me again and again that he cared about me. He had told me so many times how glad he was to have me. He told me he was happy to be with such an intelligent woman. If anything, I wanted to talk to him and find out why he would say those things. It felt fake that he would ever say those things. I couldn't even fathom the words he had spoken.

I deboarded the plane and found his truck. He walked towards me, but I couldn't look at him. I hurt. It hurt to look at him. I put my things in the truck. He got in and tried to touch my hand, but I pulled away. He apologized the whole way home. He said that he had drank too much and didn't mean any of it. He told me that my comment at dinner had made him feel insecure and then he drank too much and took it out in a way that he shouldn't have. I ended his apologies and all his words in between with, "I'll give you another chance but don't ever talk to me that way again."

Why did I give him another chance? Why allow someone who made me feel such hurt come into my life again? But what was the harm of another chance? We all make mistakes. We're all imperfect.

He looked at me with those beautiful brown eyes and I could see how much he cared. How much he didn't want to lose me. He told me he'd drink less and that he would never talk to me that way again. He said that it was disrespectful and that he would never allow anyone to say those things to his mom or sister or future daughter.

His dad called him later that day and while they talked about work, I heard his dad say, "Is everything ok with your girlfriend?"

It made me smile to know he had told his dad that he had messed up and needed to fix things.

Plans and Betrayal

Life moved forward. Day after day. Night after night. Things were busy. I hardly saw my friends. I went from school to homework to more school and homework and then from homework to work. I made time for *him*. We would spend our time working out, watching movies, cooking, and exploring the local restaurants. Always planning. Planning on trips we were going to take and then going to fly out and see some of his family. We discussed future goals and future dreams and where we would each fit into each other's lives.

The argument about me being immature, the argument about me not doing enough, and the comments on me being a slut all seemed in the past. He showed me that he was working on what he had said to me. We rarely drank anymore. We rarely went out either. He told me how much he valued me. Life was good.

He went out of town for his friend's birthday. Although I felt some apprehension, I mostly had always gone with the motto that he would do whatever regardless of what I thought or worried about. He worked hard to keep me in the loop. He texted and sent Snapchats. He told me over and over that he missed me. He made me feel secure. He was trying hard to make sure that I knew what he was doing and that he cared about me.

I went to bed one night after telling him to enjoy his night. I woke up in the middle of the night to no texts from him. I felt uneasy. I knew he was out partying. He hadn't even responded to my text telling him to have a good night. I went on social media and saw he had posted on Instagram. I wasn't upset. He was having fun. He didn't need to text me every moment. I went on over to Snapchat and that's when my heart sank. On his story he was kissing another girl.

I just stared. It was around 1 or 2 AM. The story had

been posted for about an hour. I lay there staring up at the ceiling. I had no words. No thoughts. Just sadness. I felt stupid. I felt used. I felt confused. I felt hurt. I felt betrayal. Here I was, lying in bed while he was out partying. Not only kissing other girls but putting it on his story for all to see. I felt embarrassed. I felt like an idiot. To know that anyone who knew we were dating would see that and wonder about it. They would think either we broke up or look at me and realize the pain I must feel. For those who didn't know we were together, they would think nothing of it. He had never posted me. Not even a story. Here he was posting a story for everyone to see of him kissing another girl.

I couldn't sleep. I took the pregnancy test I had been planning on taking in the morning. I figured if it came back positive, I was already in enough emotional turmoil where it wouldn't make too much of a difference. It was negative. I sighed and lay back in bed. All I could think of was the disconnect. I was at home. Missing him. Hoping he was having a good time. Taking a pregnancy test. He wasn't thinking of me. Not responding to my texts. He was kissing other girls. He was kissing other girls and posting about it.

I wasn't really sure what to do. What to say. How to feel. I felt heartbroken. Used. Embarrassed. Sad. But somehow, I wasn't shocked. I wasn't shocked.

I had begun to doze off when I got a call from him. I had no idea what he could possibly say.

"Baby. I'm lost. I'm in this guy's garage because I'm lost."

"Hm. Well your story looked fun," is all I said.

"What does it matter about my story? I'm lost in a place I don't know." He was clearly inebriated based on the way he was talking. I felt bad. He was lost and clearly very drunk.

"Well, what's the address to where you're staying?" I asked, trying to focus on the problem at hand rather than being upset. My mind wandered to why he was alone in a random neighborhood rather than with his friends, but I didn't really want to go there.

"I don't know, I thought I was near it, but I can't find it." The next hour I tried to work with him and the person who had let him in the garage to get him an Uber to where he was staying. We finally ordered an Uber, and I told him to call me when he made it safe. I felt empty though. Sad. He called again and I could hear him saying something in the background, "No, my girlfriend's getting me." He had been dropped off at the wrong address again and was wandering around a neighborhood.

"There's no need to call the cops, my girlfriend will come get me."

"Baby, where are you?" I asked.

He continued to talk to whoever was threatening to call the cops. I tried to help. I tried to call an Uber. Eventually the cops ended up coming. He made it back to where he was staying. I said goodnight. It hadn't been a goodnight.

In the morning I tried not to think. I didn't look at any of his social media as I didn't want to see him kissing another girl. It was already tattooed in my mind. I did homework and began cleaning my room. I tried to do anything that would distract me. He called me. I didn't want to answer. I did.

"Is everything all right?" he asked. I hadn't texted him in the morning as I normally would've.

"Not really. I don't appreciate your story."
"What story?"
"The one you had last night."
"What was on it?"
"I don't feel like talking about it. I'm glad you made it safe."
"Are we good?"
"I guess. I just need time."
"Tell me what I did."
"I don't want to talk about it."

We may have talked a bit longer, but I don't remember what we said. I couldn't understand why this had happened. Why did it have to happen after everything? Why did he have to post it so publicly? If I let this slide, I thought of all the people who had seen it and would wonder why I would excuse that kind of behavior. I thought of all the people who didn't even know I existed. That post made him seem incredibly single or I suppose that he were dating that girl. I didn't know what I was going to do. He continued to text me saying he was sorry, and he couldn't remember anything, and it hurt him to think he had done something to jeopardize us.

At one point he texted me and asked how I felt. I responded with, "Well imagine if I posted a video of me kissing another guy on my story and tell me how you would feel."

He didn't respond to that.

I pretended like I was fine to all my friends. I put on a plastered smile and did my best to seem happy.

"How is he?"

"Oh, he's good. He drank a lot last night." Thank god none of my friends had his Snapchat.

I was going out that night for my friend's birthday, so I called him.

"Hey, I just wanted to let you know I'm going out and I'm not mad. Just want to talk about it in person."

He said some things to me and insisted on how much he cared and how he couldn't wait to come and see me. He even Facetimed me when he was downtown with his friends to say that he missed me.

My friend said, "Wow, he really must love you."

To which I replied, "Yeah."

But how was that love? How was what we had love?

As soon as he was back, he came straight to my house. I was cleaning some more. Doing anything I could in the hopes that by cleaning I wouldn't think about it. Hoping that my mind wouldn't wander to why he was all alone in a stranger's garage instead of with his friends. Where had he been going? Where had he come from? The image wouldn't leave my mind. The video of his lips on someone else going through my head like a looped video.

He came in and sat on my bed. I continued to clean. I didn't want to say anything because then all the questions would come pouring out. Like, why would you do that? How could you post something like that? Did you cheat on me more than just a kiss? Why were you not with your friends? Do you even care about me? Or maybe not even questions, maybe something like, you've never even posted me, this makes me look like an idiot. Or, you hurt me so bad and how could I ever look past this? Or, I can never trust you if this is what you do when you're gone for a few days.

Instead, I kept cleaning. He watched me with his

beautiful brown eyes. Sadness etched into every part of his face. I couldn't help but wonder how it was fair that he was sad too. He didn't have a right to be sad. His actions had brought us here. I was the one who should be sad. *I was the one who should be sad.* I was the one who had the *right* to be sad.

He kept trying to pull me to the bed, but I couldn't stop cleaning. I could control cleaning. I could control hanging up my clean clothes and organizing my things. I couldn't control what had happened. I didn't even feel as though I could control the conversation. I knew as soon as we started talking, I would lose all control. I cared about him too much to say goodbye. I cared too much to end things. Tickets had been bought to see my friend and to see his family. Plans had been made. I knew I didn't have control when it came to him.

I could and maybe should've told him that it was over. Maybe I should've told him all the things I had thought above. But I knew that as soon as I looked into his deep brown eyes and saw the sincerity and sadness that I would lose all control. I knew as soon as he opened his mouth and started talking with his deep and remorseful voice that everything would make sense and I would forgive him.

So, I kept cleaning. Clinging to the control I knew would soon be lost. Unfortunately, there were only so many things to clean, only so many things to organize, only so many things to have control over. Eventually I had no choice but to look at him. I went and sat on the bed next to him. Not touching him. Not wanting to think of who else he had touched, who else he had looked at with those brown eyes, and especially not wanting to look at the lips that had touched someone else's. I began to cry. It felt unfair. Unfair that he would betray my trust like this. Unfair that he would make me look like a stupid girl. Unfair that we would go off and jeopardize all that we had built.

He was the one who kept hurting me. He was the one who kept saying I wasn't enough, he was the one who kept degrading me, he was the one who had left and not only done something like that but had put it on his story for everyone to see. He was the one who was hurting me. Now, he was the one comforting me. Holding me in his large arms and caressing me with his toughened hands. Telling me that he was sorry and that he couldn't lose me. Why was the one who was hurting me now trying to comfort me? He was the one who was causing the pain, how could it be that he was now the one who was easing it? Why was I letting the thing that hurt me comfort me?

"I just can't keep feeling this way. I feel stupid. I don't know how I can trust you after this. It just hurts so bad. I keep thinking about what else you might've done. I keep thinking of all the people that saw that story and now pity me and all the people who have no idea I exist since you've never posted me. But you'll post a random girl before me, and you'll even post a video of you kissing a random girl before you've ever posted something of me," I trailed off. A multitude of unspoken questions, unspoken feelings, unspoken words following behind in the silence.

"I'll do anything. I messed up and I know it. I don't even remember that night. I think I must've gotten drugged. I've been so torn up since you told me what I did. I'm so sorry. I will do anything to keep you. I will get on my hands and knees and beg you to not to let this be the end. I know I made this bed and I have to lie in it, but I'll do anything. I can change. I have shown you time and time again that I can learn from my mistakes. I won't drink anymore. I will do anything just please don't let this be the end."

My heart broke more. I felt as though every time something like this happened, he took another part of my heart away. It was as if he had a collection of the shards of my heart that he took and now it felt like I was more him than I was myself. As if he had so much of my broken heart, I no longer knew how to be whole without him. My mind went back to all the things we had done together. All the memories. All the laughs and smiles. How could it be the end? How could it be the end when we had so many plans for our future together? How when we had flights booked for only weeks away?

He kept saying how he couldn't lose me. How I was the only person who had ever understood him. He kept telling me that what we had was special and that when you meet someone who understands you and you enjoy them, you shouldn't let them go. He asked me to forgive his mistake because we all make mistakes, and he told me that one day I would make a mistake and how could I throw away what we had knowing that inevitably we all make mistakes.

I looked in his brown eyes and I listened to his low voice, and I let his large arms hold me. I felt as though I didn't have control. I couldn't say it was the end. Why? I don't know. I loved him. He said he loved me. If it really was just a kiss, how could I even allow myself to be all that upset?

The weeks that followed were perfect. We laughed together, smiled together, supported each other in our day to day lives. He made me dinner and told me how amazing I was and how much he cared about me. He told me I was the sweetest thing he had ever met.

He always said things like, "You really are the nicest person I have ever met. You truly don't want anything more than to be loved."

He understood me. Perhaps that's why I couldn't let it go. I was a broken individual. The scars of my past etched into every part of me. The hard memories of childhood. The feelings of being taken advantage of in adolescence. The feelings of sadness, dirtiness, and lack of control that I had always felt. And he understood me. He understood me better than anyone else ever had. He wasn't like the guys in my past who had never really seemed to understand why I was the way I was. They would try to listen, try to understand, but they could never fully understand.

Maybe he understood because he was equally as broken as I. Maybe two damaged people could make a whole. Maybe if you loved each other enough you could look past the brokenness and the mistakes and hold onto that person. Because to be completely honest, sometimes I felt as though he might understand me better than I understood myself.

Almost every night I fell asleep in his arms. My body pressed against his. I could feel his heartbeat against my back and could hear his breath in my ear. I felt safe in his arms. Safe from the world and safe from my past. I would wake up almost every morning to lay on his lap as he got ready for work. He would kiss me on the head and then quietly leave and oftentimes he would come back in to give me one last hug and one last kiss before he went about his day. I would wake up to good morning texts and he would check on me throughout the day. We would shower together in the mornings sometimes and he would put the body wash all over me and rub me clean.

He always prayed in the morning. He would pray aloud while I was with him in the shower or after I had already gotten out. He wasn't ashamed to say them aloud. He would thank God for the day ahead and he would thank God for his family and his friends and his health and the health of his family and friends. And then he would thank God for me and tell God how amazing I was and how blessed he was to have me in his life.

He would encourage me about school and visit me at work. My coworkers all thought he was amazing.

"He is so manly."

"He is so large."

"He is so driven and hardworking."

"He is so sweet to you."

And my friends would say things like,

"He treats you really well."

"You guys seem so happy."

"You guys have a lot of chemistry."

"He is so thoughtful."

"He really makes you laugh."

I would tell him what I was stressed about, and he would listen. I could cry about inconveniences, and he would hold me. I would tell him some days that I was sad and didn't know why and he would say that's ok I'm here for you and I'm proud of you. He would tell me about work and his goals and sometimes he was so tired after work that we would just lay together. He would doze off and I would look at him as he slept, and he appeared so innocent. Not a care in the world. Face not creased by worry or anger. I thought about how we all are a little messed up. A little imperfect. Maybe love was finding someone who accepted you for your brokenness. Maybe love was loving someone despite their brokenness. Maybe by loving someone you were able to become a little more whole.

I looked at him as he slept, and I thought about how we all were once children and sometimes we were hurt as children and that creates who we are now. When he slept, I couldn't help but think of the hurt boy he once was. I was once a hurt girl. Now we were both broken adults trying to find our way through the world. Each making mistakes. Each saying things we didn't mean. But in the end, we understood each other and were there for each other. Maybe that was love. Understanding the other and being there for them no matter what. Being there for them despite the brokenness, despite the ugliness, despite the mistakes.

Family, Sacrifices, and Sickness

It was finals week, but my professors had done this thing where they all said, "Since you'll be so busy next week, I have the final scheduled for class time this week." I had finished my finals in all except one of my classes. He had mentioned that he was going to drive and visit his family that lived a few hours away. I said I would like to come. And we went.

He drove and I sat next to him. We talked, we sang along to music, and I laid my head on his lap. As we pulled into town, I told him to stop by a grocery store so I could get some wine as a present for his mom. He picked up flowers. He always brought flowers for his mom and younger sisters. He brought me flowers a lot too. He brought me flowers often enough to where I always had fresh, beautiful flowers. He never let them wilt.

His dad and him had a meeting so I hung out with his mom. She asked how we had met, and I told her. She asked about my family and my degree, so I told her. I did my best to make a good impression. I am slightly shy though, so I never know if I've made a good one.

When we got back to the house he was back. Him and I jumped on his trampoline, and he gave me a tour of his childhood home. Pictures of him and his family were strung all over the walls, a collection of memories and moments. It was precious to see him younger. He was such a cute kid.

Him and I headed to the mall for a bit and then went to get martinis. We sat and talked and drank our martinis. It felt right. To be there with him. To meet his family and then head off on our own for a while. He took me to my favorite restaurant and then we headed back to his house.

I helped his mom cook for a bit. Him and I drove and picked up some pizza for his siblings. We looked at the Christmas lights and sang along to Christmas music. When we returned the kids quickly ate their pizza and I helped clean up after them. I remember his mom saying, "Look at her cleaning up, she's a keeper."

I wanted to be a keeper. I wanted his family to like me. I wanted his younger siblings to get to know me to the point where they asked about me when he went and visited without me. I wanted his mom to ask for my number so she could text me. I wanted his dad to tell him what a nice young lady he'd found.

After the kitchen was cleaned up, he and I looked through his baby book with all the old pictures of him. His mom watched us and commented on the photos. She told me embarrassing stories about him. I laughed with his family, smiled at him, he beamed at me, and everything felt right. Everything felt exactly as it should be.

We had to get up early since I worked at 7 AM, and his family lived a few hours away. It was blizzarding so hard that we had to trudge through deep snow just to get to his truck. He kept telling me to call in but for whatever reason I refused. I don't know why. He told me he didn't mind driving anyways but that I should call in because they'd understand. But to me, going to work was important. Even in a part time job I felt the need to be a good employee, to show up, to feel as though I had my freedom. Given the snow, I should've probably called in.

It was pitch dark. The snow was coming down at a speed that made it difficult to see. I kept telling him how grateful I was. He had even been vague about why he was leaving early when his dad asked. I assumed it was because he didn't want his dad to dislike me for making his son get up at 4 AM to drive in a blizzard for a part time job that hardly paid.

We talked about our future, about our hopes and dreams, we talked about friends and family. We talked about everything on that drive. Our words floated into space just as the snow floated down from the sky. All there was, was black sky, white snow, black road, white swirling all around. And him and I and our words and our dreams and our promises. Our words passed by just as the snow did. There one day and then melted the next. True one day and then gone the next. Just as snow falls, remains, and then melts. So, promises are spoken, hang in the air, and then are gone. Not untrue just as the snow itself is not untrue. The snow is there one day and then just as quickly disappears. Likewise promises are spoken and then eventually gone. Naturally gone, melting into oblivion like the snow that melts as time passes on.

We finally made it back to my house. I texted my work telling them I'd be late. Then, they texted me saying I didn't need to come in. The look I gave him when they sent that text. We could've spent the day with his family. Instead, I made him drive me back in the dark in a blizzard. I couldn't believe I had found a man who would do that for me. He knew I enjoyed working and so sacrificed time with his family to get me there just for me to be called off. Not to mention that he hadn't told his family I was the reason we were leaving. What an amazing man. I was happy to call him my own.

I had a final later that day. Then he and I went and celebrated with drinks. I didn't feel particularly well so we headed back to his house and watched a movie. I was happy that I got to meet his family. I was happy that we had been able to spend the day together. I was happy.

The next day when I woke up, he was already at work. When I sat up, I immediately felt nauseous. I went to the bathroom and threw up. I texted him and told him I wasn't feeling good. A half hour later he was back with ingredients for soup. He spent time with me all day despite how sick I felt. I couldn't even talk, I felt so nauseous. Whenever I opened my mouth, I was afraid I would throw up. He took care of me. He rubbed my back, filled a bath up for me, made me homemade soup, and held me tight.

All I could think about was: This is finally it. This is the relationship that I've been waiting for and have always wanted. A man who takes me to meet his family, a man who makes sacrifices to make me happy, and a man who leaves work to take care of me while I'm sick. I was so relieved. To finally have found love. To finally have found someone who was giving me what I was giving them. I had found someone who wanted me, someone who wanted to take care of me, someone who wanted a future with me. Someone who made me feel whole despite the brokenness, someone who loved me despite my past, someone who loved me despite my imperfections. Someone like *him.*

Damaged

"Do you love me?" I asked him as I lay in his arms.

We had said it multiple times in the past, but the moment was perfect and him saying it would make it even more perfect. I was laying in his arms. Naked and vulnerable. His large arms wrapped around me. The only things clothing me. The sunlight filtered lazily through the window. It was early morning. Nowhere to be. Just us.

I thought of how I wouldn't mind spending the rest of my mornings like this. His arms caressing me. His warmth seeping through me. He was kissing me. Kissing my hair. Kissing my neck. Whispering in my ear. His hands made their way slowly down my body. I felt safe.

"Do you love me?" I said with a smile. His kisses marked invisible tattoos on my body and his arms held me as if they were the only things keeping me together.

He flipped me around, so I was facing him. I couldn't wait to look in his eyes and feel his body against my nakedness and hear him say those words.

"I do love you…" he said, and my body sighed and slowly melted into his. My eyes got lost in the brownness of his. I never wanted to stop looking in those eyes. I never wanted to stop feeling his arms. I never wanted to stop hearing those words come from his lips.

I smiled as he said them. I knew more words were coming with the way he spoke the, "I do love you." I looked at him and waited for the next ones.

"But…" With that one single word my heart sank. My body pulled back. The safeness in his arms dissolved. I once again felt broken. I once again felt alone. I once again felt insecure. One word and I felt all the pain I had ever felt before. All the uneasiness came crashing in. The uneasiness that sometimes slipped through what appeared to be a perfect relationship.

"But I don't know if you really love me," he finished. I felt the hurt reflected in my eyes as he spoke those words. I did love him. More than I had ever loved anyone else. More than I thought maybe I should sometimes. Those words hurt. Those words stung. Those words seemed to strip away everything I had been working towards with him.

"Why do you think I don't love you?" I asked. My voice felt small. Why was I constantly feeling smaller and smaller?

"Because you've been with other guys and how

would I know that you aren't saying that just as you have with others? Besides, I feel like you're lying about the number of men you have been with. I can't be with someone who a bunch of other men have had access to."

I remember the world freezing and my body seizing and my heart hurting. I remember wondering why me asking if he loved me in a teasing way had led to this.

"I don't understand what you mean. We both have pasts, but I don't think those should matter. What matters now is how we treat each other and how we build this relationship."

"So you're not going to answer my question about how many guys you've been with?"

"I have told you, but I also don't see why it should matter."

"It does. I can't be with someone who has been with a bunch of people."

We'd had this conversation before. I had also explained my past in the hopes he would understand why I am the way I am.

Months ago, I had told him, "When I was younger, I was sexually assaulted."

I don't remember why I told him. It was late at night when we were talking about life and our pasts, and I had started crying. I guess I told him because I wanted him to see me for who I was and am. I explained the dirtiness that stayed after. He wiped away my tears and told me that I was beautiful regardless. That he wishes he could've protected me from that. He told me that it made him sick to think about someone touching me at such a young age. He understood my brokenness because he had experienced what it feels like to be broken as well.

I had told him how I wanted to wait for the right person to have sex and how my first boyfriend told me he would wait for as long as was necessary. He told me he liked me for me and not just for my body. Then he texted his ex to sleep with him since I wouldn't sleep with him.

Then I began to believe that men would only ever want me for my body. That my body was the only thing that made me valuable to them. The only thing that would make them want me and made them stay with me.

They didn't like me for me, they wanted my body. The only way to get attention from men is to give them your body. That ideation began to form in my brain. Men only want me for my body.

I had told *him* that and explained that due to my reasoning I had lost my virginity to a man I met over the summer. Yes. Man. I was 16 and he was significantly older. I had thought that by having sex with him, he would date me, love me, and he would want me. I was wrong. He left me. Men might only want me for my body. But maybe that's not enough to make them stay.

I had told *him* about the TV static and the basement and the party and the unwanted touch. I had told him it all in the hopes he would understand me.

Now, here *he* was. Telling me that just because I had a past and been with other guys that *he* couldn't be with me. Couldn't be with someone who had been used by men all her life. I thought back to all those times I had been used.

The times when nos had been ignored and the please stops had been muffled and the I don't want tos forced right back down my throat.

"You are a liar," he told me. I was dirty to him. I was damaged goods. I was broken beyond repair. Dirty beyond the ability to ever be clean. Used and left and unwanted.

And although the conversation started with me asking if *he* loved me, it now changed into me being a liar. Being too used for him to stay with me. Him telling me that my past was my fault. He said to me,

"You put yourself in the position to be used. You're telling me that you were assaulted by guys to make yourself look like you're the victim so I will stay with you. You wanted to have sex with them. You put yourself in the position and you probably wanted it at the time. You are a liar. You lied to me and you're lying to yourself," he spoke the words with such venom. Such hate. A man whose family I had met, a man who I had shared life with, a man who had met my family, a man who had told me he wanted me to move in with him. And he hated me. Hated my past and who I was. After everything we had built and been through. I was not good enough. I was too used to being of any use to him.

"I am not a liar." My voice broke and the tears wouldn't stop. "I went to a guy's house when I broke up with my ex my freshman year. But I had told him before I went there that I didn't want to sleep with him. I was lonely. I just wanted to hang out and watch a movie. Not that it matters because even if I had said I wanted to have sex with him I still would've had the right to say no. I kept saying no and no and no and no and he kept ignoring me. Yes, maybe I shouldn't have gone over there in the first place, but I thought that we had an understanding. We were just supposed to hang out. I never said yes. I said no. Regardless this was before I had ever even met you. I don't understand why it matters. We all have pasts. You have your own. I love you regardless of your past. It's about creating a future. It's about accepting someone despite the things they have done and experienced."

"You are delusional. Now get out of my house."

He had to drive me home. I didn't have my car. I kept pleading with him. Telling him that my past shouldn't matter. Telling him that lying about being assaulted is a terrible thing, something I would never do.

They had never believed me. After that party when I was younger. I had told my friends. They didn't believe me.

"You've hooked up with him in the past. Besides you were drunk you probably just don't remember."

But I did. I did remember. I remember saying no. I remember not wanting to. I remember trying to push him away. I remember what it felt like to have him push his way inside of me even when I had said no. I remember feeling cold. Empty. Damaged.

He told me I was lying. That I was a slut. That I was damaged.

Was I lying? I shouldn't have been at that party when I was a teenager. I shouldn't have drunk so much. And in college, I shouldn't have gone to his house so late. I should've known better. We had been talking but I shouldn't have gone over so late, and I should've insisted on us going to the movie theater rather than meet at his place. It was in part my fault. I should've never put myself in those situations. It was my fault. I was a liar.

"I'm so sorry. You're right. I should never have put myself in those positions. I guess I know that you wouldn't want to be with me because of it," I said. Feeling so small. So damaged. So dirty.

"You're right. I can't be with someone who puts themselves in that kind of position. You lied to me because you knew I couldn't be with you if I knew the truth."

"I'm so sorry. I love you. I just want us to move on and focus on our future," I kept saying that to him over and over.

He finally pulled over. "I love you," he said. "Despite your past. Despite your lies. I'm probably the only person who will ever love you despite the lies you've told. You're right, it's about the future. It'll take me some time to get past this though." He pulled me close and kissed me. "I love you," he said again.

He loved me despite my dirtiness. Who else would accept me despite my past? He was right, how could anyone else love me? I was too dirty to be loved. I couldn't even love myself. He loved me and he knew all there was to know. He loved me despite my brokenness. He understood me. Who else would understand me the way he did?

I know I couldn't love myself. I didn't love myself. I was a slut. I once was 15 and wanted to wait and then I began to believe my body was the only reason men would ever notice me. I was young and naive. I should never have believed those things. Never let men have access the way they did. I was dirty and broken and damaged. How could anyone ever love someone like that? It was my fault the things that had happened to me. But he loved me anyway. *He* loved me.

I look up from the set of practice questions I was working on. The difference between when to use 'habría' and 'hubiera' had my brain hurting. I wish I had learned Spanish at a young age. I thought about moving to Spain permanently. Then I would have no choice but to become fluent.

I stared out the window of the coffee shop I sat in and thought back to *him* and what he had said. We live in a society full of double standards. Double standards where men can sleep with who they want, when they want, and society doesn't bat an eye. "He's just being a man." If anything, being older and still a virgin as a man is considered unusual. The more sex the manlier the man.

Women on the other hand are considered either pure angels or dirty whores. They should be experienced but not *too* experienced. Sexy but still innocent. If women sleep with too many men, they are considered "loose," sluts, and they "sleep around." If they don't do anything with a man, they are prudish, a tease, and not "putting out."

I had a past. We all do. He held my past over me. He told me I was a liar. Convinced me that I was liar. Lying about being used.

Consent can be a slippery slope. In school I watched a video about tea. Comparing tea to sex. That may sound ludicrous but, in some ways, it creates an analogy of what consent looks like in a more lighthearted manner. In the video they talk about making tea for someone. If the person declines tea, in what world would someone force tea down their throat? If someone were passed out, why push tea down their throat? Someone might even invite someone over for tea and then once they get there, decide they don't want tea with them anymore.

Unless someone says, "Yes, I would like tea." Why would you make them have tea? Why would you convince them to drink tea? Why would you ask over and over and over to drink tea? Unless it's an enthusiastic yes, then don't make them drink tea.

My heart hurts for those who have been silenced. For those who were told they were liars. I wish that I could talk to everyone who has ever second guessed themselves or been convinced that they are not the victim but the one to be blamed.

I wish I could reach out to those who were hurt when they were younger and give them a hug and tell them it will be ok. I wish I could change society and the double standards that are etched into the lives we live. I wish I could change my past to something prettier, something purer, something a little less dirty, and a little less complicated.

I wish that I had let him leave. He was looking for someone I wasn't, I can't hold that against him. I wish I had known that you can't change your past, so find someone who accepts you for it and not hates you for it.

I look back at my page, "Si me (hubieras/habrías) dicho, te (habría/hubiera) ayudado."

It's Your Fault

Early in the relationship I had told *him* how I felt about cheating. After the cheating rumor that surfaced at my birthday, I told him that cheating was the one thing I would never make an exception for. I explained that my ex in college had messaged his ex asking her to come over the day before he met my dad. I knew the girl and she had told my friend that he reached out to her. I found this out weeks after he met my dad.

To me, messaging someone is cheating. Not in a messaging a girl about anything kind of way. I mean messaging a girl and clearly messaging them with the intent of doing something with them. Some may disagree but I consider flirting and messaging about meeting up to do things cheating. I had told *him* this and he had agreed. I even had told him that my first boyfriend had done the same thing. Messaging an ex when he and I were together. Messaging her about meeting up with him and hooking up with her.

I had both of his birthday gifts all wrapped. Sitting in my room. They perched on my desk like two birds, bright, and colorful, and ready to be opened. His birthday was later that week. He and I were just hanging out and talking. I had an open evening for once and he had gotten done with work early so we could spend time together. I appreciated that he had done that. He had even taken work off in the past to spend time with me. It was thoughtful and I appreciated him making time for me. We were discussing summer. Summer when I would be living with him.

"I love summers here. They're beautiful. I've never been in a relationship during the summer. I'm excited," I said as we discussed hiking and swimming and enjoying the summer sun.

"That's funny," he replied in a way that made me

know that he did not find it funny at all.

"Why?" I asked confused.

"Just because winter is cuffing season and then relationships end in time for summertime."

"I mean, I've just never had my relationships make it to summer. I guess with my ex we spent some time together, but he never really came down to see me during the summer," I explained. Realizing that my comment hadn't been all the way factual. *He* often got upset with me for telling half-truths or not explaining a situation fully. I wanted to avoid a conversation where I was called a liar.

"I thought your ex and you broke up because he cheated."

"Yeah, it's a bit more complicated than that. More or less, I heard that he had messaged that girl, but he lied and told me that she was just saying that. There wasn't any proof and I wanted to believe him. Then I found out from one of his friends that he indeed had been intending on cheating on me. I found out he had lied the whole time and then he never came and visited me really over the summer, so I broke up with him."

"You must've really loved him to get back together with him when he cheated on you."

"Not really. I just didn't actually think he had intended on cheating on me and then I found out that he actually had been."

"Yeah, but you wanted to believe him. You cared about him enough to where you didn't want to believe the truth."

"Maybe. But mostly I hadn't realized the full situation."

"You know, you always tell me how you've been treated badly in the past, but I really think that if you have someone cheat on you and you take them back then at that point it's your—" I cut him off.

"If you're about to say it's my fault that men cheat on me or my fault that I get treated unfairly by men then you might as well go," I said and pointed to the door. Maybe I should have reacted differently to his comments, but we had a very similar conversation earlier that week. Two somewhat similar conversations on two very different things.

I had been explaining how my friend had met this guy and how they had been on a few dates, and he talked about how much he liked her and enjoyed her company and how he would love to date her. Then they hooked up and he stopped trying. Stopped texting her as much and then not at all. Stopped following through on their plans and then not making any at all.

She texted him and said something along the lines of, "I'm busy and I know you are too. I don't really feel that this is moving forward unfortunately given that I continually tell you when I'm free and we make plans and then you don't follow through."

He sent a text in return that said something like, "I'm sorry you feel that way."

My friend was hurt. She felt used that someone would tell her all those lies just to use her and ghost her.

Then, months later, he messaged her again. He messaged her on Valentine's Day. They started texting again. Bantering. Joking around. Just like they had the first time. He said he really wanted to take her on a date and try again and that he was truly sorry how things had ended last time.

She told him, "Look I really enjoy talking to you but I'm not just looking for a hookup. I like what we have and want someone who will take me on dates. I want you to take me out and see where this can go rather than just hooking up."

He told her, "I would love to take you out on a date. I want to take you on so many dates. I want to make it up to you."

Then, they went on a date. Eventually they hooked up and he never talked to her again. She found out weeks later that he was texting another girl the entire time and was dating that girl now.

I had told *him* this. He had been with me many times when she had called me to cry and wonder why he had done those things. Why did he lie when he could've just told her the truth. Why had he wasted her time? Why had he used her like that without any care for her emotions.

Some may ask, why did she go back to him after what happened the first time? I'll go ahead and ask, "Why would someone treat someone like that in the first place?"

Some may say, just as *he* said, it's her fault. She should've known he would do the same thing again. She shouldn't have given him another chance. To which I would say. He shouldn't treat women that way. He shouldn't lie. Men shouldn't treat any woman that way. *Him* and I had agreed to disagree. I had been irritated that he thought of it that way but didn't want to argue.

So now, here he was. Telling me it was my fault. That it was my fault that men treated me the way they did. It's my fault they cheated on me. My fault for taking them back. Maybe I overreacted. I most likely should've taken a deep breath and used some "I statements." I statements being when you take responsibility rather than blaming the person you're talking to. Something like, "I feel upset when you call me a liar" or "It hurts my feelings when you say it's my fault I have been cheated on in the past."

Maybe I should've said, "Hey, let's talk. Those things really hurt me. Being cheated on really hurt me. I feel really disrespected when you say that it's my fault that men have done those things to me."

I should've said those things. But I was fed up. Fed up with his, "You must've really loved him to take him back. You don't love me like that." Which brings me to the second thing we had already talked about the week before.

We were watching the new rendition of *West Side Story*.

Just after my favorite song "America", he looked at me and said, "Do you even like me? You've dated men in the past and allowed these men to have access to you that you won't even let me."

I started to cry. I cry a lot I suppose. He brought this up as earlier in the day when I had gotten to his house, I hadn't felt like being intimate with him. "Why would you say that? I just didn't feel like being intimate. I had a hard day at school, and I have a lot on my mind. Besides, that's unfair to say that I have allowed others to have access that you don't. It's my body. It has nothing to do with previous relationships or this relationship. It's my body and when I want to have sex I will say yes and when I don't, I will say no."

"Yeah, but I want to have a girlfriend that wants to have sex with me. I bet you would never do this with your ex."

"This has nothing to do with relationships in the past. I don't want to have sex. It doesn't mean I don't care about you as much; I just don't want to do those things right now."

I could continue with the dialogue but to be completely honest we went in circles. Him accusing me of not loving him because other people in my past were given more access to my body than he was. To which I would reply that other relationships had nothing to do with anything and that I would rather he be respectful and understand that it's my body and I will do what I want when I want and when I'm ready. It kept going. Circling and circling, over and over. Repeatedly. I felt like a hamster stuck continually on a hamster wheel. Never getting anywhere, never gaining anything, just seeing the same wheel and running over the same parts over and over again.

Eventually he said, "I'm leaving."

I hadn't stopped crying the entire time.

"Where are you going? You don't work for another hour," I said.

To which he replied that he was going to one of his friend's houses. I stood up and walked to his front door before he could leave, I had to get to class anyways. I descended the steps and got in my car. I wanted him to follow me. To apologize. To say that he was wrong. Because how could he be saying those things? In a relationship someone shouldn't pressure you to do things you don't want to do. I should've stayed and said, "Listen, I don't agree with what you're saying, and I feel disrespected by what you're insinuating. I am going to class for now, but we can continue this once we've had some time to think things over."

But I didn't. I walked out the door expecting him to follow. He did but he went to his truck. I stopped backing up my car, waiting for him to apologize. He stared at me with a steely expression. No emotion. Nothing on his face. I laughed. I couldn't help it. Who shows no emotion when arguing?

He misread my laughter as me not being upset anymore and came and sat in my car. We continued to argue when eventually I told him to get out of my car before I was late to class. Talk about healthy communication.

As I drove away, he texted me saying that he couldn't do this anymore and that he would grab his stuff from my house. I responded with something like, "How would you let something like this destroy everything that we've built." Because that's what relationships are. Something you build. Love isn't just an emotion, it's an action. Something that you must continually decide to work for every day. The initial strong feeling of love essentially fades over time, but actions remain there. Each day in a relationship takes conscious effort.

I sat through my class heartbroken and confused. Why would someone end a relationship over something like that? Didn't he care about me? Wasn't our relationship more than sex. Wasn't it about our conversations and experiences and all the dreams we had?

I got out of class to a text that said he was sorry and that he was sorry if I felt disrespected and that we would figure it out. He told me had made dinner and that he had tea ready and that he loved me. He called me and told me to come over so we could talk it out.

I went to his house. We continued our "conversation" and continued with the same circles we had been going in before. Him being upset that I wouldn't have sex with him whenever he wanted/ I cared more about my ex because I probably had sex whenever he wanted with him/ I didn't give him as much access to my body as I had with my ex. And I responded with how disrespected that made me feel/ it's my body/ that it was unfair to say that if I loved him, I would do those things.

At one point I told him, "You make me feel afraid. You make me afraid that if I don't have sex with you that you'll just go and have sex with someone else. You make me afraid that one day I won't, and you'll make me. You make me feel like your love is conditional. I don't feel respected by you."

I spoke out of anger, hurt, and confusion. Who says those things? Love isn't defined by sex. Love isn't demonstrated by allowing your partner to do whatever they want when they want. Love is shown through mutual respect. Love is shown by making your partner feel safe and protected. Love should not be measured by how much you do for that person but the realization that each person is doing as much as they can for that person because they care about that person and want to make them happy.

In response he said, "If you feel that way why don't you just leave? Why would you be with someone who makes you feel unsafe and disrespected?"

As I responded my voice broke, "Because I thought you'd change. Because I didn't think you'd ever make me feel those things." As I said those words, reality hit in a way. Why was I with him? Why was I with someone who made me feel those things? Why would I believe that he would change?

You should never be in a relationship thinking that you can change someone. 1) People don't change. 2) If you need someone to change to be with them, you don't love them. Because that's who they are. You can't love someone you think they may be able to become. You need to love them for who they are now.

I grabbed my backpack. Ready to leave. Still not wanting to leave though. Why? Because I couldn't understand it. How could this person tell me they loved me? How could they tell me that they wanted a future with me? How could they say they wanted me to move in with them just to say that I don't love them enough and that I don't love them because I won't do whatever they want when they want. This was not the man I had thought he was. He was not the man who had told me early on, "You are an incredible woman. You are smart. You are sexy. You are so hardworking. You are going to do so many amazing things. I am sorry about the way you've been treated."

This was not the man who had taken care of me

when sick. This was not the man who made me dinner and made sure I had eaten. This was not the man who took me to see where he was from and meet all his family. This was not the man who told me who couldn't wait to meet my parents.

As I grabbed my backpack about to leave, he said, "Don't go. Come here. We'll figure this out." He guided me back to the bed. He held me close. "We will figure this out because we love each other, and we care about each other. I let him hold me. I felt small. I felt broken. I stayed.

And now, here I was, pointing at the door. Telling him to go if he was going to finish that sentence. Because he had told me that it was my fault men treated me badly. Because he was telling me that I didn't love him as much as those in my past because I wouldn't do whatever he wanted and that I loved my ex so much more because I would stay with him even when he cheated. *He* did leave. He walked out the door.

I texted him and I texted him. I texted him about how disrespected I felt and how it was wrong for him to tell me it was my fault. He eventually called and asked if I'd calmed down. I responded that no I had not. I told him that he shouldn't have left.

He said, "I'm going to leave if you tell me to."

To which I said, "I told you to leave if you were going to finish that sentence."

The conversation basically turned into me telling him that he should come over to my house again so we could talk it through. He said he didn't want to. He told me he didn't want to see me.

I told him that I didn't think that was a good idea

and that I thought he should come over and we'd have issues if he didn't. That wasn't right of me. If he needed time, I should've given him time. I shouldn't have threatened him like that.

I told him that what he said was wrong and that I felt disrespected and that I was upset that he had left and that he should come back so we could talk about it and figure it out.

He came back. I apologized. I apologized for reacting the way I did. I said that I was trying to stand up for myself and had felt disrespected and that I was upset that he would even say something like that. He told me he didn't want to touch me and that I was still in love with my ex and that I would never care about him the way I did about my ex and that I talked about my ex too much. He got up to leave. I was confused. The conversation had begun about summertime and how excited we were for summer and suddenly had turned into a fight about how I loved my ex since I took him back after he cheated and that I was still stuck on my ex. All I had wanted to do was set boundaries. All I had wanted was to stand up for myself for once.

Now he was leaving again. Walking out the door. Telling me he couldn't be with someone who was still stuck on their ex. I looked at him.

"I'm not still on my ex."

"You talk about him a lot."

"I don't mean to. You just get mad because I don't tell the whole truth or the whole story. So, I've been trying to get better about that. When I mentioned summer, I didn't want you to think I was lying, I wanted to tell the whole truth about how I was in a relationship, but he wasn't around much."

"I can't be with someone who doesn't treat me how I should be because they're still into their ex. You've let him do things with you that you haven't let me."

"You don't even know that." The next part of the conversation got continually more and more confusing and convoluted until he called me a liar about something.

"I'm leaving," he said and walked to the door.

I got off my bed and blocked the door. I took deep breaths.

"Listen, if you don't like me anymore or you're not attracted to me anymore or if you don't want to be with me for another reason that's fine. But why would we end this over my ex. Someone I don't care about anymore. Don't make it be over that. It's not true. I don't think about him anymore. I have told you about him only when you've asked. Or when if I didn't mention him, you would say I wasn't telling the whole truth. You get upset when I don't tell the whole truth but when I do you say I talk about my ex too much. If you feel that way, I'm so sorry but I truly don't mean to. I just told you things in the hopes that you'd understand why I am the way I am."

I begged him to stay. I wouldn't let him walk away. I wouldn't let him leave. I told him if he were going to, he should take his gifts too. He said he wouldn't. I opened his gifts and threw them at him. "Here are your gifts. Take them. I do care about you. I just want to be able to celebrate your birthday and you meet my parents. I don't want to fight, I never wanted you to feel the way you feel. But if you're going to leave, take these gifts. Because I do care." I shouldn't have thrown the gifts. I shouldn't have forced him to stay.

He took the gifts without looking at them and put them back in the wrapping bags. He lay in the bed. He told me he'd stay. I don't remember much else from that night. Just feeling confused and hurt and sad but relieved that he had stayed after all.

What is Love?

I lay on the beach. The only sound being that of the waves and the wind. I'm in Spain. Sometimes I forget. Sometimes I forget about *him.* Or I guess I forget the absence of him. I'll get a text and expect his name to pop up just to remember that it won't. It never will again.

What is love? We sing about it, read about it, dream about it, and sometimes believe ourselves to be experiencing it. We talk about love as if we know what love is, what it looks like, and what it feels like. But what is love? Is love forgiving someone no matter what? Is love forgiving someone even when they don't deserve it because you love them so much? Is love staying with someone despite the things they have done, simply because you love them? Is love making exceptions because you want them to be in your life forever? What is love?

How can you tell someone loves you? Is it when they make sacrifices for you? Is love when someone drives in a blizzard in the dark for you? Is love when someone puts you first, even before work or themselves? Is love shown by the things you buy them? It is measured by the number of flowers you give them? Is love shown by the number of texts they send in a day? Do you know if someone loves you because they always bring you things you love? Is love when they make sure you've eaten? Is love shown by cleaning? Is love shown by how many times you do their laundry or how many times you clean their dishes? How do you know that someone loves you?

How do you know when you love someone? Is it when you want to spend all the time you can with them? Do you know you love someone when you feel yourself changing things you never thought you'd change for them? Do you love someone when you make sacrifices, sacrifices that you're not even sure you should be making? Do you love someone when you're so afraid of losing them that you do anything that you can to keep them, even if that means doing things you wouldn't normally do? How do you know when you love someone?

We live in a society where love is portrayed everywhere. Love is shown in advertisements whether that be in commercials, on billboards, or in magazines. Love is demonstrated in movies and books even when the love that is depicted is not healthy. Love is sung about by people who have love, or have lost love, or are looking for love. Love is everywhere and yet what is love?

Is love even love if it's unhealthy? One could argue that the TV show *You* shows love. There are two individuals who will do anything for the other, including murder. Is that love? Because if so, what is that telling us? It's telling us that if you love someone you will stop short of nothing to "protect" and "demonstrate" that love. No matter what mistakes the other individual makes, no matter how bad the fighting, no matter if cheating occurs, no matter what, love is still there and should not be let go of. I have a hard time believing that is love.

Or consider the movie *365,* the entire premise is that this woman falls in love with the man that kidnaps her. The idea is that love happens unexpectedly, and that love can come from any circumstances. And what does that tell us? Regardless of whether someone watches the movie and believes that to be love or not, deep down an idea begins to form that, love forgives and forgets. Who cares that this man took her away from her friends and or family? Who cares that he took away her freedom? He cares about her, and she cares about him and that is what love is about.

Consider the book, *Gone Girl*, a woman creates an entire persona in order to get a man to fall in love with her. She creates her personality to be that of someone he would fall in love with. Then, she slowly begins to show her true self. In the book she tells him that she is the only woman he could ever love because without her he would be bored. She challenges him with the idea that she is the only woman who truly loves him, she literally became a whole different person for him. Despite the lies, betrayal, and manipulation, in the book he even admits at one point that perhaps she is right, perhaps she is the only woman he could ever love. That brings about this idea that to love someone means to change yourself or at least manipulate them in the process.

The typical premise of a book or movie about love

is the following: Boy and girl meet, they spend time together, they begin to like each other, they realize they have feelings, either the boy or the girl lied about something or does something that pushes the other person away, they miss each other, eventually the one who messes up seeks out the person and tells them that they can't live without them, they make up and begin a life together. The overall idea is that if you love someone enough, you will forgive them because the alternative is living without them.

But that's not real life. Sometimes you need to walk away. Sometimes that person never apologizes. Sometimes the other person can't forgive. It's not as simple as: Meet, hang out, figure it out, resolve any issues, happily ever after.

How are we supposed to know what love is if everywhere around us are examples of what love isn't or what love is only partially?

I saw this post thread online about this girl and her boyfriend. She tells him she's going to hang with a friend, when he finds out she's hanging out with a guy friend he tells her that he "owns her" and "didn't give her permission." I looked at the comments below and they all talked about how they would love to have a guy like that. "He cares about her so much" or "Where do I find a guy like that."

I thought about my own experience. Having to change whole plans with my friends if other guys were around. Not being able to text guys I had been friends with for years.

I keep thinking about that thread. How is that healthy? I can't imagine that level of control is healthy. "I own you." I don't think that's what relationships are. You don't own your significant other even when you marry them. You are joined together by commitment and if you care about that person, you will never do anything to hurt that person intentionally.

In my own relationship it began with him being upset at me for responding to a guy classmate or responding to a guy friend. Both men had no interest in me, they were simply my friends. Would I hang out with them one on one, no. Would I reach out first, no. He told me that, "All guys want is to get with the girls they are friends with."

I suppose he was right given that's what he wanted to do. But the difference is, regardless of whether they wanted to, I would never encourage behavior like that because I have a boyfriend and am committed to him. That's the difference. It didn't matter what their intentions were because I was faithful to him. It began like that. He got so angry that I was responding to other guys. It felt a bit restrictive, but I complied and oftentimes ignored well-meaning texts from my guy friends because I didn't want to get in trouble.

Then things segued, it wasn't just, "You can't respond to your guy friends."

It became, "Why would you hang out in a group when other men will be there?"

Sometimes someone loves you and you love them, but the love shared isn't healthy. It doesn't mean they are a bad person, or you are a bad person, it just means that together you don't bring out the best in each other.

There are two sides to every story. I am an unreliable narrator and hindsight is 20-20. I loved him and at the time I thought that was enough. He wasn't a bad man. There was so much good, there were times he treated me better than I could ever have imagined, nights when I thought we would never stop laughing, and sacrifices that he made that meant the world to me. There was good, so much good. But we both acted in "bad" ways when together. I did bad things and said bad things too. But sometimes just because you love someone doesn't mean you should stay. It's hard to walk away, it can be scary to walk away, but when you begin to lose sight of yourself, all you can do is leave. Sometimes it's better to forget the good and remember the bad in order to walk away.

So, what is love? I still have no idea what love is. I have loved and thought I have loved and been loved and thought I have been loved. It's important to remember that someone may truly love you, but not be treating you the way you deserve. If that's the case: Leave.

The End

I have been busy enough the past few weeks to hardly think about the past except for bits of time here and there. I sit on a couch in the window room at the apartment in Spain and I work on a presentation that I have tomorrow.

I have been doing my best to forget that night ever since it happened. I have done everything I can to block it out and erase it from my memory. I set down my homework and look out of the window to the street below. As much as I don't want to remember it, any of it, especially that night. The street slowly dissolves, and I am in *his* room that night. That night.

"My brother will be in town soon. Are you sure you don't want to come out with us?" I asked as I lay with my head on his chest.

"I'm sure. I have to work early. Go have fun with him," he responded. Things felt weird. I didn't know why. I didn't like the feeling. I had been having this feeling for a while. A feeling of suffocation. I didn't feel like I could breathe. And when I did, breathing hurt.

I got my brother from the airport and kept texting *him* asking if he would come out. He kept declining. Something felt wrong. I felt tense, nervous, and unsure why.

My friends and I were out at the bar with my brother when *he* showed up. He bought a drink and talked to my brother, and I felt like I could breathe a little more. *He* kept trying to dance with me, but I kept telling him I wanted us to talk to my brother, besides I felt uncomfortable dancing with *him* in front of my brother.

"I'm gonna get a drink." *He* walked away.

He didn't come back.

I went to the bathroom. *He* was talking to another girl. I don't mean talking, I mean he knew her and was *talking*. I felt upset. We all left the bar.

Things got *blurry*. Things got blurry for all of us. We later found out we had been roofied. All I can remember is me crying. Me talking to *him*. *Him* disappearing. My brother trying to comfort me. Me getting pushed to the ground. Taking an Uber. Texting *him*.

-Where are you?

-Where did you go?

-We are going home

-I just got pushed to the pavement. Where are you?

I continued to text *him*.

-Where are you?

-I need you.

I look at his location. He's not at his friend's house, he's not at his house.

-I hope she's worth it.

In the morning. I got a call from him.

"Hey is everything ok?"

"Everything is ok."

But was it? Where had he been?

The day is a blur. Turns out being roofied isn't much fun and it turns out the day after being roofied isn't much fun either. Him and my brother chatted and laughed, and we all went out to eat. I slept with my head in *his* lap while he stroked my hair and they talked. *He* had apparently lost his phone, lost his keys, and didn't know where his truck was. He had stayed at his friend's house the night before. I told him his keys and phone were probably there. I told him I had his location, and we could go get his phone. He said we could get it later.

Him and my brother drank champagne. A lot of it. My brother went to shower. *He* became mean. He had drunk too much. He told me that he wondered if my brother knew that I was a slut. He wondered if I had ever told my brother of who I truly was. I told him to leave. He kept talking. Being rude. Continuing to say hurtful things. He ordered an Uber off my phone. He had no car, no keys, no phone. Off he went.

"He really loves you," my brother said. "He told me about all he has planned and that he'll do whatever it takes to have you in his future."

I didn't feel like replying. I went on Snapchat instead to see if I could Snapchat his friend about his phone. Except it wasn't my Snapchat. It was his because he had logged in to mine earlier that day to text his friend off my phone.

And in a moment, everything can change.

All the lies you have been telling yourself can change.

All the moments can be ruined.

All the I love yous disappear.

All the promises and everything in between can melt away just like the snow.

There were two girls on his Snapchat. Although I was told I couldn't Snapchat guys because all guys want to do to is get with their friends…

I click on one of the messages. I see months of messages between them. Not just conversations. Graphic questions. Dirty texts. I screenshot.

The next one is from a girl he must've been with the night before. While I was home with my friend and brother, He was with her.

I text him even though I know he doesn't have his phone. I send the screenshots and in one sentence I end a year's worth of promises and futures and beginnings. I text him: Never talk to me again.

It's midnight when he calls off an old phone. He still doesn't have his phone. He doesn't know I know. He hasn't seen the screenshots I sent. I ask him if he's ok, I ask him if he has what he needs to get his car back. Then I tell him. Silence. Then crying, excuses, empty words, broken promises, and all the lies in between. I hang up.

A knock on the door. He tries to explain. He tries to apologize. Tries to tell me that it isn't what it looks like. Tries to tell me that I'm wrong. That he loves me. That he wants a future with me. That he can't imagine life without me. I don't care, I tell him to leave.

He drops off my stuff with a letter. Tears on the letter. He says he never cheated. He says he wants a home with me and a child and a future. He says all the things he has always told me. This time though I don't see those brown eyes and fall deeper in love. This time I don't imagine the amazing memories and beautiful times we spent together, and I can barely envision a future anymore, rather I see the end. I can finally breathe.

Part 5
Growing

Spain: Present

I now sit on a rock in Spain overlooking the ocean. Just as the waves crash in and out of the shore so my thoughts undulate. Crashing with memories of the past, the present and the future. All melding together. There is no distinct past, present, or future just as the receding waves mix in with new ones so does time. It's hard to differentiate the past without thinking of how it impacted the present and impossible to imagine the future without considering everything that comes before it.

I think back to the basement and the TV static and being played with. I think about who she was. She no longer feels like me. She seems like someone else. My heart hurts for her, wanting to protect her and knowing deep down she will always be within me. A hurt child. A trampled blossom.

I think back to when I was growing, growing despite the dirtiness, despite the brokenness and how it felt to be touched without want. Without wish. The feelings of being dirty once again.

I think back to *him*. I thought that he loved me despite my brokenness, despite my dirtiness. Maybe he loved me. But his love hurt. Not allowing me to forget the scars of my past but rather making it even more impossible to move on from them.

I think of myself now. Sitting here. Trying to escape it all. Trying to let distance, ocean, and newness wipe away the old. Despite the distance between me and them and him and all the past, the past is just as much a part of me now as it was then. I can't escape the memories as hard as I try. I can't escape the feeling and emotions and dirtiness and emptiness and betrayal. That being said, I'm healing. Growing again. Replanted and waiting for roots to take to the soil.

The thing with flowers: no matter if they die, no matter if they are dug up, no matter if they are trampled or picked, or thrown away. They never stop being beautiful.

The thing with growing. It takes time. It takes sun and rain and patience. And sometimes it looks as though the flower is dying or dead or drying up, but eventually it blooms and grows and spreads.

I am healing and it takes time. It has taken then and now, and it will continue to take time. But I am finally growing again. Despite the dirtiness that sometimes never goes away, despite the pain that sometimes never fades. Despite it all, I am moving on, healing, growing out, growing up, and despite it all stronger than I was before. I am growing. I am healing. I hope you can too.

About the Author

Sarah Miller is an author who has enjoyed reading and writing from a young age. Growing up in Colorado, nature has always been an important part of her life, therefor imagery and the interactions between humans and nature is an essential part of her writing. Graduating with a Bachelor's Degree in Science and an emphasis in mental health, Sarah strives to write with the intention of creating conversation as well as tackling societal topics, gender norms, and challenging perspectives.

www.ingramcontent.com/pod-product-compliance
Lightning Source LLC
LaVergne TN
LVHW041851070526
838199LV00045BB/1542